"Are y[illegible]
Daddy say[illegible]
me all bett[illegible]

Angie smiled, her pixie nose crinkling, her hollow eyes showing a sparkle of delight.

"Well, um, no, I can't really—" Emma answered.

Mark frowned, then took Angie's hand. "Come on, honey, we've got some other doctors to visit today."

He led Angie to the door. The little girl clung to one of his fingers, her hand small and vulnerable. He turned to give Emma one last desolate glance. She didn't like watching him beg. Nor did she wish to see him lose his daughter.

"It was good to see you again, Emmy," Mark said.

"But, Daddy, I thought you said Dr. Shields would take care of me. What'll we do now?" Angie asked in a loud whisper.

Emma closed her eyes, squeezing tears between her lashes. What had she gotten herself into?

"Wait, I forgot I had a cancellation. I can see you next Tuesday."

LEIGH BALE's

debut novel, *The Healing Place,* won the RWA's prestigious Golden Heart Award for Best Inspirational Romance in 2006. A member of Phi Kappa Phi Honor Society, Leigh also belongs to various chapters of RWA, including the Sacramento Valley Rose; the Faith, Hope and Love Chapter; the Hearts through History Romance Writers, and the Golden Network. She is a mother of two wonderful children and her son is a U.S. Marine. Leigh lives in Nevada with her professor husband of twenty-six years. When she isn't writing, Leigh loves playing with her beautiful granddaughter, serving in her church congregation and taking history classes. You can visit her Web site at www.LeighBale.com.

The Healing Place
Leigh Bale

Published by Steeple Hill Books™

STEEPLE HILL BOOKS

ISBN-13: 978-0-373-87462-0
ISBN-10: 0-373-87462-6

THE HEALING PLACE

This edition published by arrangement with Steeple Hill Books.

www.SteepleHill.com

Printed in U.S.A.

Then they cry unto the Lord in their trouble, and he saveth them out of their distresses. He sent his word, and healed them, and delivered them from their destructions. Oh that men would praise the Lord for his goodness, and for his wonderful works to the children of men.

—*Psalms* 107:19–21

To Steve, Daniel and Marie, for standing
firmly against the maelstrom.

Also, my undying gratitude to Dan and
Marjorie Baird, Steve Burnett, Bill and
Clara Howard, Gary Jackson, Ren Johnson,
Wayne Johnson, George Keele, Koret Family
House, Michael Lehners, Make-A-Wish,
Alan Mentzer, Sue Ross, Justice Thomas Steffen,
Peter Umphress, Dennis Widdis, and Doctors
Mitchell Berger, Jay Chamberlain, Kathy Eckert,
Michael Edwards, John Shields, Joseph Walker
and their staffs. Thanks for being there.

Chapter One

Reno, Nevada

She couldn't face going home tonight. Dr. Emma Shields scribbled notes on the last patient's case file before she set it on top of the stack to be sorted by her office staff. She peered at the brass clock on the wall and blinked. Was it really that late? No wonder she was bleary-eyed. She sighed and returned her attention to her work. Anything to delay going to her lonely apartment.

A short knock sounded on the open door.

"Come in," she called without looking up.

"You plan on staying here all night?"

Emma lifted her head. As she removed her reading glasses and dangled them from her fingers, she sat back in her comfy executive chair.

Too comfy. She stifled a yawn.

Sonja, her head nurse, stood in the doorway, prim and proper in her whites with red stars stamped on her smock. Sonja smoothed her graying hair and showed a crinkly smile.

"Nope, I'm about finished," Emma replied. "What's keeping you here so late?"

"I got those pathology reports you requested from Dr. Tanner and sorted them for tomorrow. You've already got your messages, so I think I'll call it a night."

"Good night." Emma reached for another pile of paperwork stacked neatly on her desk.

Tidy and in control. That's what her receptionist called her. Emma couldn't help that she liked order. She'd had enough chaos in her life to last an eternity.

Sonja turned to leave, but paused. "Oh, before I forget, Mr. Williams called again."

"Mr. Williams?" Emma shook her groggy head. "Remind me."

"He has the little girl with a brain tumor. He's called twice this week. He's asked if we'll work with his doctors at the University of California Hospital in San Francisco, to administer her chemotherapy protocol."

"And did you tell him we deal only in adult oncology?"

"Yes, but he says you're the doctor most highly recommended by Dr. Meacham, his neurosurgeon."

"Larry Meacham?"

"None other."

An impatient huff escaped Emma's lips. "The next time I see Larry at a medical convention, I'll have to remind him I don't take pediatric cases anymore."

Not since I lost Brian.

Sonja didn't budge and Emma found it difficult to hide her irritation. "Where's the tumor located?"

"It's on the hypothalamus."

Not good. The hypothalamus was a pea-size gland that told the pituitary gland what to do.

"Inoperable?"

Emma didn't really need to ask. She'd seen it before in adult patients, time and time again, but this was an innocent child. God could be so unfair.

A rush of bitterness swept her. She'd grown comfortable with her anger and no longer tried to fight it.

Sonja nodded. "Yep, so they're starting chemo."

"What drugs will the child be on? How often do they need to be administered?"

"I'm not sure. He didn't say."

Emma tilted her head, longing to remove the too tight clip at the back of her neck and free her long hair. "No, I don't want to take this patient."

I can't work with another child with cancer. I just can't.

"But it's so sad, Dr. Shields. The little girl's a baby—only six years old."

Emma's heart squeezed. Brian had been five.

She shook her head. "I'm very sorry, but administering drugs to a growing child is a lot different than dealing with adults."

"But she's been through so much already. She had her first surgery here in Reno, then they rushed her to U.C.S.F. for a biopsy. She's had several more surgeries since then, to drain cysts and install a VP shunt. Her father's agreed to begin a chemo protocol as soon as he can find an oncologist. You know there isn't a single pediatric oncologist in this city."

Yes, Emma knew. "But there are five other doctors in Reno that specialize in adult oncology. Refer Mr. Williams to one of them."

Sonja quirked her brows. "He's already tried and they said no. If you'll let me, I'll take full charge of overseeing her protocol."

Emma almost groaned. Certified to administer chemotherapy drugs, Sonja was one of the best nurses at her job. She was also too generous. A widow and grandmother of two, Sonja had been Brian's nurse when he had been ill, caring for him tenderly, reassuring Emma that everything would turn out all right.

It hadn't turned out all right and the night Brian died, Sonja had sobbed as bitterly as Emma.

Sonja smiled gently. "Losing ourselves in service to others is a great way to lift our own pain."

A shadow of remorse crowded Emma's mind. She served many patients every day—her bank account swelled with the results. But what good was money when she had no one to spend it on? What service had she done recently, just because someone needed her? Just because she could?

Nothing came to mind. Not since Brian. Because he blamed her for their son's death, Emma's husband had left her, too. Their marriage had been rocky long before Brian got sick, but the loss of their child had finished it. God had taken everything from her and then abandoned her.

No wonder I feel so lost and alone.

Her gaze shifted to a plaque on the wall, a wedding gift from her mother, three months before her death. Written by Adam Lindsay Gordon, it read, "Life is mostly froth and bubble, but one thing stands as stone. Kindness in another's trouble; courage in one's own."

Emma crossed her legs and clasped the armrests of her chair. Courage? Kindness? She was fresh out of both.

She peered out the window at the evening sky, a darkening blue with tinges of pink and orange as the sun tucked itself behind the western mountains. Hadn't she tried to do the right thing for Brian? And look what that had gotten her.

The death of her child, followed by a painful divorce.

"It would be so easy to help them," Sonja prodded, undeterred by Emma's frown.

"I said no."

The words dropped like stone. This wasn't her problem, nor her responsibility. God had put her through enough already.

Emma heard Sonja leave and she stared at the closed door. She couldn't go through that hurt again. It was that simple.

The next afternoon things weren't as simple as Emma hoped. Standing in the hallway of her medical office, she paused beside the closed door of an examination room to study the blood readings for her last patient of the day. Over the low hum of the busy office, she picked out Sonja's voice coming from the front reception area.

"I'm sorry, Mr. Williams, but it's like I told you this morning on the phone—Dr. Shields has such a heavy patient load already, it wouldn't be fair to Angie."

Angie. Was that the child's name?

Emma paused, listening. She could hear the strain in Sonja's voice. Sonja didn't want to reject Mr. Williams, but Emma had given the nurse no choice.

"Have you tried Baker and Calloway's office?" Sonja suggested another oncologist.

"Yes, and they refused. My neurosurgeon said Dr. Shields is the best, and that's who I want for my daughter."

Mr. Williams was *here?* This fellow was *not* taking no for an answer.

As she stood in the doorway of her office, Emma saw Sonja sitting at the reception desk, looking up at a man who leaned against the counter. He had his back to Emma, holding an enormous envelope of files beneath one arm. No doubt the envelope contained various pathology reports and MRIs from his daughter's neurosurgeon. It looked like he had brought *everything.*

Dressed in navy-blue slacks and a light yellow pinstriped shirt, he was tall and slender, with shoulders wide as Texas. His short, slicked-back hair reminded her of the color of damp sand. He shifted his weight and shoved one hand into his pants' pocket. His stance tensed. What if he caused a scene?

"I need to see Dr. Shields. If I could just talk to him—" Mr. Williams's voice sounded low, edged with desperation.

"*Her,*" Sonja corrected in a kind tone. "Dr. Shields is a woman."

Mr. Williams lifted his hand in a gesture of frustration. "If I can just *talk* to her for two minutes, I won't take more time than that."

Like a coward, Emma ducked into her office and leaned against the wall. Her pulse throbbed, her hands clammy.

"Please. If I have to beg, I will."

His beseeching tone touched the deepest corners of Emma's heart—what little she had left. She squeezed her eyes shut.

Opening her eyes, she swallowed and clenched her

teeth. If she said yes this time, it would be harder to say no to the next parent who walked through her door. Brian's death had cured her of taking any more chances.

She stepped around the corner and pasted a professional look on her face. As she walked toward Mr. Williams, she extended her hand. "Mr. Williams?"

He turned.

She froze. No, it couldn't be.

"Mark? Mark Williams?" Her voice sounded watery to her ears.

When he saw her, his eyes widened and his features softened with relief. "Emmy! Emmy Clemmons. Wow! How long has it been?"

She tried to pull her hand back, but he caught it and squeezed tight. The warmth of his fingers tingled up her arm.

"Uh, it's Shields now. *Emma* Shields." She emphasized her first name. It had been two years since anyone had called her Emmy.

He smiled but it didn't reach his eyes. "You must have gotten married. So, who's the lucky guy?"

She ignored the question. "Your daughter has a brain tumor?"

"Yeah, she needs an oncologist. Are you the *oncologist?*" Amazement creased his brows and *finally* he released her hand, which she put behind her back.

He rubbed his angular jaw where a day's worth of stubble showed he hadn't shaved that morning. He was thinner than Emma remembered, but faint lines around his eyes showed increased maturity and fatigue. Regardless, he was still handsome as ever, with the power to break any girl's heart.

He looked good. Too good.

"Yes, that's me." Her voice sounded strangely robotic.

Oh, *why* did this man have to be her former high school boyfriend? They'd dated for about a year and then he'd dumped her for Denise Johnson, head cheerleader, a.k.a. The Doll. That's what all the girls called Denise behind her back because they were so jealous of her long blond hair and perfect good looks. They hated Denise because all the boys loved her.

Mark shifted the envelope of files beneath his arm and shook his head. "You know, I wasn't surprised when I heard you went to med school. You were such a bookworm in high school and always wanted to be a doctor. I knew you'd go far."

Yeah, when Brian died and David left, she'd almost gone off the deep end.

"Emmy, we need a good oncologist. We need *you.*" Mark's voice sounded firm, insistent.

Emmy. She hated that name.

Overhearing the conversation, Emma's receptionist threw her a curious glance. As she directed another patient into the treatment room, one of the nurses gave Emma an inquiring look. The attention bothered Emma. Why couldn't her staff mind their own business?

"Let's go into my office where we can speak in private." Emma stepped back to lead the way.

"Okay, but—" Mark shot Sonja a quick look.

"I'll bring her to you as soon as she's finished in the bathroom," Sonja said.

Oh, no. The little girl was here, too. This was *not* going to be easy.

Mark followed Emma into her office. In anticipation

of the arrival of his daughter, she left the door ajar before she rounded the large desk and sat down. She was grateful to put some kind of barrier between her and Mark.

He sank into one of the three chairs facing Emma's desk and leaned forward, his fingers clasped, elbows resting on his knees. His gaze locked on her and he appeared confident and in control, the same old Mark she remembered from high school.

"You look great, Emma. How've you been these past fifteen years?"

She threw a fleeting look at him, then stared at the black stapler on her desk. "I've been fine."

"Do you and your husband have kids?"

She wasn't about to tell him about her sweet son or her nasty divorce. "What line of work are you in, Mark?"

"I'm a CPA. My firm serves mostly local contractors. It's busy and lucrative."

It probably suited him, she thought. As a kid he'd lived in a mobile home on the "other" side of the tracks. With his dad gone, his mother had worked hard to eek out a living for them. All he'd ever talked about was marrying a beautiful girl and making truckloads of cash so he could live a life of style and ease. It looked like he got his wish.

"So, how's The Doll?" she asked.

He sat back. "You mean, Denise?"

She tried to laugh, to lighten the moment, but it sounded more like a hoarse croak. Her hands were damp and she felt the sudden urge to run from the room and hide. "Yeah, remember? That's what we all used to call her."

He shook his head. "No, I never called her that."

"Oh."

Was her foot too big to fit inside her mouth?

"We're divorced." He spoke in a vacant tone but she caught a flicker of pain in his expressive eyes.

Inwardly, Emma sighed. As a doctor and a mother, she understood the strain a child's critical illness inflicted on a marriage. She had learned that lesson the hard way.

"I'm sorry." And she meant it, for the child's sake.

Anguish filled his eyes, then was gone. Though she had never liked Denise Johnson, she felt bad Mark's marriage had failed.

Emma shifted in her chair. She didn't want to feel bad for this man. She didn't want to care about him or the chaos in his life. She needed him out of her office and out of her life.

Fast.

"Look, Mark, I'm not going to pretend. I can't take your daughter on as a patient. I've already got more than a full load and it wouldn't be fair to you or—"

He shook his head before she finished speaking. "I can't accept that, Emma. Angie's been through so much. If you tell me no, I'll be forced to drive ten hours round-trip to San Francisco every week. My partners said they'd cover for me, but I don't think Angie can take the exhausting drive. She has little energy and no appetite. It'd be better if she gets her treatments here in Reno. Can't you take her as a patient, just for old time's sake?"

Angie. What a sweet name.

"No, I'm sorry, but I can't. My staff isn't prepared to deal with a child's growth and hormone issues."

His face fell, his eyes hollow with defeat. He no longer appeared in control. Instead he looked vulnerable and lost. "You're kidding, right?"

He sounded as though he really couldn't believe her.

"Mark, I know the limitations of my office."

He ran a hand through his hair, making it stand on end. "Look, Emmy, I'm…I'm desperate. I'm afraid if you don't help, I'll lose Angie. I can't risk that. She means everything to me. Please, I'm begging you. Don't turn your back on us."

He breathed deeply, as if the words had been difficult for him to speak, and she supposed they were. She'd never seen Mark Williams beg for anything. As the senior class president and campus jock, he'd been self-absorbed and conceited. What had changed him? Parenthood, or perhaps something more?

A lump formed in Emma's throat and she knew irrevocably that he loved his child, just like she loved Brian.

She stood, prepared to walk him to the door. "I don't think—"

"Daddy?"

A little girl poked her head into the room. Seeing Mark, she walked over and climbed into his lap. Sonja stepped in long enough to smile at the child and close the door, giving them complete privacy.

As her gaze swept over Mark's daughter, Emma almost panicked.

Angie. No doubt, when she was healthy, she'd be a stunning beauty like her mother. A miniature image of Denise, with small, pert features, wide eyes and silky blond hair. Or at least, from the long braid at her temple, Emma thought Angie's hair was blond. Most of it had been shaved off, though she couldn't tell for sure because the child wore a white hat with pink-and-blue flowers on the front.

It was obvious Angie was sick. She was all eyes, surrounded by shadowy circles. Her thin face looked pale and her spindly arms and knobby knees seemed so slight a puff of air could have blown her over.

Just like Brian in his last days.

The image of her son ravaged by illness still haunted Emma. She wished she could erase the cruel memory from her mind.

Angie snuggled close to Mark. He wrapped his arms around her and kissed her cheek, breathing deeply of her warm skin.

"Everything okay?" he asked Angie.

"Sure." She responded in a small voice, her gaze never leaving Emma.

There was such poignancy in watching Mark with his daughter that it brought a throbbing pain to Emma's chest. How she missed the feel of her son in her arms, his simple prayers at bedtime, his warm kisses good-night. Even her ex-husband's constant criticism hadn't bothered her then.

An overwhelming impulse to help protect Angie rose up inside of Emma. She tightened her hands, forcing herself to resist the urge.

Mark made the introduction. "Angie, this is Dr. Shields."

Angie smiled, her pixie nose crinkled, her hollow eyes showing a sparkle of delight. She lifted a frail hand and fingered the end of the long, thin braid at her right temple. "Are you my new doctor? Daddy says you're gonna make me all better."

Thanks for making this tougher, Mark.

Emma clenched her fingers around the armrests before she answered. "Well, uh, no, I can't really—"

A horrible, swelling silence followed.

Mark frowned and looked away, coughing as if he had something stuck in his throat. Finally he patted Angie's leg and stood, taking her hand. He wouldn't meet Emma's eyes. "Come on, honey, we've got some other doctors to visit today."

He led Angie to the door. The little girl clung to one of his fingers, her hand small and vulnerable. He turned to give Emma one last desolate glance. If she didn't know better, she would say he looked near to breaking down in tears. She'd never seen him cry and never wanted to. His tortured expression injured the deepest recesses of her resolve. For all her desire to have him get his comeuppance for dumping her all those years ago, she didn't like watching him beg. Nor did she wish to see him lose his little daughter.

As Mark twisted the doorknob, a sinking of despair filled Emma. Urgency built within her to help them.

"Thanks for your time, Emmy," Mark said. "It was good to see you again."

He sounded desolate. Emotion played across his face. Grief and—

Fear.

How many times before Brian's death had Emma felt those same emotions?

"But, Daddy, I thought you said Dr. Shields would take care of me. What'll we do now?" Angie asked in a loud whisper.

Emma flinched. She couldn't open her heart to more hurt, or let herself worry about this child. God would only let her down again.

The truth was she feared what Mark and Angie could

make her feel. What if she came to care for them? The little girl would most likely die and Mark would blame Emma for it. She couldn't stand to face that again. Not after all the horrible things David said to her at their son's funeral. Yet, if Emma refused them, she wouldn't be able to live with herself.

In spite of her loss, the Hippocratic oath she'd taken after medical school jangled inside Emma's head. She had to look beyond her own pain and remember she was a doctor, first and foremost. Her conscience and self-respect wouldn't allow her to do otherwise.

Emma closed her eyes, squeezing tears between her lashes. Something buried deep inside warned she would regret this, but the warm feeling in her chest told her it was the right thing to do. "Wait! I, uh, I forgot I had a cancellation. I can see you next Tuesday."

Mark's mouth dropped open and he stood patiently while Emma gathered her thoughts.

"Bright and early Tuesday morning," she continued. "That should give me enough time to contact your doctor at U.C.S.F. and find out what protocol we'll be administering."

A wide smile split Mark's face and his hazel eyes sparkled. Laughter rumbled in his chest, the deep sound of rolling thunder. "Emmy, I don't know what to say. Thank you. We'll be here."

Mark squeezed Angie's hand and inclined his chin toward Emma. His expression showed relief. "You see, Angie-love, I told you not to worry your pretty little head. Everything's gonna work out fine."

The girl flashed a smile at her father. "Yeah, and she's pretty, too, Dad."

Winking at Emma, Mark pivoted and left. Emma stared at the closed door, pressing her shaking fingers against her trembling lips.

"Oh, no," she whispered. "What have I gotten myself into?"

Chapter Two

Mark tossed another load of laundry into the washing machine, then wiped off the granite countertops in his kitchen. The tiled floor felt sticky where Angie had spilled her cherry punch and he headed for the pantry to get the mop. As he filled a bucket with hot, sudsy water, he leaned against the refrigerator and stifled a yawn. With two corporate tax returns for clients due tomorrow and Angie's first chemo appointment in the morning, he'd be lucky to get three hours of sleep tonight.

After he mopped the floor, he skimmed his fingers along the elegantly carved balustrade of the spiral staircase and went upstairs. The thick Berber carpet muffled his steps. He and Denise had chosen nothing but the best for their spacious home. Growing up in a shabby trailer park, he'd spent hours of his youth dreaming of living in an elegant home like this. Now, he'd give it away free if it would heal Angie. The realization that all the money in the world couldn't make his daughter well again caused him to change his priorities. Maybe he should sell the place and buy a simple three-bedroom house he could maintain more easily.

He'd think about that tomorrow.

Hopefully, Angie was ready for bed. At bath time, he hadn't rubbed her head too hard because it was so tender from stitches—two hundred and thirteen so far. Angie kept count. Battle scars, she called them.

Poking his head into her room, he found it dark, except for a reading lamp on the nightstand by her bed. Stuffed animals crowded the top of her dresser. Books and trinkets lined two shelves, including a small jewelry box with a dancing ballerina on top and an orange ceramic bowl she'd made in first grade. He loved every one of the drawings and finger paintings she had plastered on her walls. A jump rope, skateboard and hoola-hoop stood propped in one corner. Even if she had the energy to play with these toys, Mark didn't dare let her for fear she might fall and jar her head. The last thing they needed was another surgery.

Angie sat up in bed, staring at a picture of her mother beside the clock radio on the bedside table.

"Hey, honey-girl, it's late. You should be asleep." He smiled, remembering the first time he'd caught her with a flashlight under her covers, reading a Trixie Belden book; advanced reading for a kid barely out of kindergarten.

Her brow furrowed as he sat beside her on the bed. He brushed his knuckles against her temple. "Something wrong?"

"When's Mommy coming home?" A single tear trickled down her cheek.

Regret swamped him when he thought of all the woulda', shoulda', coulda' things he might have done to keep his marriage alive. He hated that Angie had to pay the price for her parents' failure.

"Remember, Mommy's gone to stay with Grandma."

He couldn't bring himself to tell her Denise now lived with another man. According to Denise's mother, the guy was still in college, twelve years younger than Denise. The kid had taken Denise to Europe and the Bahamas, while Angie spent her days with doctors and specialists.

Anger crowded Mark's mind and he tried to fight off the resentment. He wasn't ready to ask God's forgiveness for these emotions, but without God, he believed he would fall apart. And he needed to remain strong, for Angie's sake.

"Mommy may come to visit us, sweetheart, but she won't be living with us anymore." He'd told Angie this before, but she couldn't seem to accept it.

Neither could he.

Heavenly Father, where are You? How much more can I bear?

In the quiet, Mark heard a still small voice speaking within his soul.

I'm here, son. I've never left you.

"But why doesn't she call us?" Angie asked, her bottom lip quivering. "Doesn't she love us anymore?"

He scooped Angie into his arms and hugged her tight. As he breathed deeply of her warm, sweet skin, he tried to calm his troubled thoughts. "Of course she loves you. Maybe Mommy's extra busy and hasn't had a chance to call."

Yeah, right. Too busy with the preschooler to call her sick daughter.

Their dogs, Tipper and Dusty, curled up beside Angie—no barking or wagging tails. It was as if the hyper Maltese and toy fox terrier knew Angie was ill and they protected her the only way they knew how.

"Can we call her?" the child persisted, snuggling deeper beneath the flowered comforter.

He'd tried to reach Denise numerous times, but his ex-mother-in-law refused to give him the new phone number. "I've already called your grandma and asked her to tell Mom you want to talk to her."

Thanks, Denise, for leaving me to figure out how to keep from breaking our daughter's heart.

Angie sighed, with relief or sadness, he wasn't certain. "Is she mad at me? Because of the brain tumor?"

"*Nooo,* honey!" He cupped her pale cheek with his hand. "It's not your fault Mommy left. You had nothing to do with it. She's fine. I don't want you to worry about her, okay? Just think about getting better."

"Can't you be friends again?" Angie suggested. "Maybe you could say you're sorry and Mom would come home."

If only it were that easy.

"We would both have to want that, and right now, Mommy doesn't."

In all honesty, he didn't want it, either. Not after the pain Denise had put him through by leaving him for another man.

Angie nodded, her hollow eyes a haunting remnant of the bouncing girl she'd once been. He'd give anything if it were him who was sick, instead of Angie.

"Dr. Shields is nice," she told him.

He flashed her a smile. "Yeah, Emma always was

nice. And very smart. She knows just what to do to help you get better."

What a blessing they had found Emma. The moment he'd seen her standing in her office, he'd felt complete trust in her abilities. Though she'd been reluctant to accept Angie as a patient, Mark had no doubt God had sent them to her. With her help, and through God's grace, they would get Angie well again. He refused to believe anything less.

Mark fingered the thin braid at Angie's right temple. His throat clogged with tears when he thought of how kind the nurses from Angie's last surgery had been, making a big deal over an inch-square of long hair because it was all Angie had left on her head. The neurosurgeon had shaved the rest off, replacing it with a melee of stitches.

"Don't worry, Daddy. It's gonna' be okay," Angie whispered and patted his hand.

Mark blinked. *She* was comforting *him?*

The center of his being swelled with hope. If she could have faith, then so could he.

He kissed her cheek and murmured against her ear. "I love you, honey."

"I love you, too, Dad."

Tears blurred his vision.

Please, God, don't take her from me. He prayed the words over and over in his heart.

"What's up for tomorrow's schedule?" Angie yawned, her eyelids drooping.

"Tomorrow, we go see Dr. Shields for your first chemo injection."

Mark had decided not to keep things from Angie.

She had a right to know what the doctors were doing to her and why.

"Don't worry, Dad. I'll be brave."

Emotion washed over him and his throat felt like sandpaper. She was the bravest person he knew. "Of course you will. Now, are you ready for prayers?"

Because he didn't want to jar her too much, he resisted the urge to tickle her like he used to. Instead he knelt beside her bed and waited while Angie folded her arms and began speaking in a hushed voice.

"Heavenly Father, thank You for Tip and Dust and our house and Dr. Shields. Bless Mommy and help her come home soon, and help Daddy and me be brave. And help my tumor die. In the name of Jesus Christ. Amen."

"Amen." Mark opened his damp eyes. "Now, lay back and close your eyes again and imagine the tumor in your mind." He paused, giving her time to begin their nightly ritual—a suggestion from their neurosurgeon. "Can you see it there in your mind?"

"Yes," she whispered.

"And can you squeeze it tight and see it getting smaller, and smaller, until it just disappears?"

"Yes." A soft murmur. "It's almost gone."

"Okay, kill it, honey. Kill it and tell me when it's dead and gone."

Long moments ticked by as he watched her brow furrow with concentration.

"There. It's all dead." Opening her eyes, she gave him a smile so bright that a lump formed in his chest.

He held her for several minutes, just because he could, just because she was alive and warm and here in his arms, and one day she might not be—

He wouldn't go there.

When he saw that Angie was asleep, he pulled the covers to her chin and backed out of the room and went to sit in the dark family room.

Alone.

No lights, no television, no wife. Just him, staring at the time flashing on the DVD player until it blurred and he had to blink.

His hands trembled and his breathing quickened. A hoarse cry rose upward in his chest. Cupping his face with his hands, he leaned his elbows on his knees.

Tears flooded his eyes and he wept.

Chapter Three

"Please, take a seat. Dr. Shields will be here shortly." Sonja directed Mark and Angie into an examination room.

"Thanks, Sonja." Mark pressed the palm of his hand against Angie's back, urging her to sit on the vinyl couch, which had a fresh pillow in a stiff pillowcase lying at one end.

A short stool on wheels and one chair sat beside the bed. The room smelled of antiseptic. Jars of cotton swabs and alcohol wipes rested on the counter beside a small sink. Perched beside the door, a magazine rack held the latest issues of the *Wall Street Journal, Newsweek,* and various parenting magazines.

Angie settled on the bed while Mark slumped in the chair and stared at a picture on the wall. A ski slope in winter. Aspen, maybe.

Feeling Angie reach over and slip her hand into his, he sat up straighter and squeezed her fingers tight. She wore a worried expression and he gave her a reassuring smile. "Don't be afraid. You've got the EMLA Cream on and it shouldn't hurt at all."

Thank goodness their neurosurgeon had given them a prescription for a tube of EMLA. The cream's topical deadening powers worked wonders the numerous times Angie had to be stuck by a needle.

She nodded, but he sensed her tension. He'd lost count of the needle pokes she had endured. She had never become immune to the pain.

Neither had he.

He wished he could take her place and do this for her. It helped him understand how God must feel as he watched his children down on earth, struggling through their trials.

Sonja opened the door and came in carrying a tray with a hypodermic and a vial of amber liquid. The nurse set the tray on the counter, then prepared the injection.

"The doctor will be right in." She spoke in a cheery tone.

Mark coughed. "Sonja, how long have you worked for Emma, er, Dr. Shields?"

Sonja chuckled. "I've known Dr. Shields long enough that sometimes even I slip up and call her Emma. I met her in a science class at the university when she was an undergrad. I went back to school after my husband died, so I was kind of old to be a student. Emma and I were lab partners. I introduced her to her former husband, David."

"Former?"

Sonja's eyes creased with sorrow and she shook her head. "I'm afraid they divorced two years ago. It was pretty hard on Emma. David never was a very supportive husband."

Mark's insides went cold. He understood firsthand the sadness caused by divorce.

He was about to ask more, but Emma opened the door and came in, carrying a clipboard. Dressed in a white blouse and black skirt, she wore a white doctor's jacket over the top, buttoned mid-way up the front. Her blond hair was pulled back in a tight knot at the base of her neck. She wore wire-rimmed glasses low on her nose. Even with the severe hairstyle, he remembered how stunning she could look when she let her hair down and smiled.

The moment she entered the room, he felt as though he'd come home. Safe. Like a breath of fresh air after being locked in a tiny closet for six months. Her presence soothed his jangled nerves, offering hope in a weary world of fear.

Old feelings of affection crowded his heart. Wow, it was good to see her!

His gaze darted to her left hand where a gold wedding band circled her fourth finger.

How odd.

She'd been divorced two years, yet she still wore her ex-husband's ring. After two years, he would have thought she would be over the guy. He was definitely over Denise. He realized his priorities had changed since Angie's birth, but Denise hadn't changed one bit. Somehow, the distance between them had grown to unrecognizable proportions.

Mark looked away but couldn't help wondering if Denise had hocked her garish wedding ring at a pawnshop. No doubt, she could get a tidy sum for the diamonds.

At one time he hadn't cared. Now he wished someone in this world loved him enough to wear his ring. But even if he found that special someone, he doubted he'd have time to build a relationship. Angie was his first priority and kept him more than busy. He couldn't afford the luxury of a romance right now.

"Hello." Emma glanced at him, then turned to smile at Angie.

"Hi, Emma." His voice sounded unusually low and he cleared his throat.

Pen in hand, Emma sat on the stool and began scribbling notes on her clipboard. "Angie's blood count looks good right now. This blood test was performed yesterday?"

She peered at Mark over the rim of her glasses, her clear blue eyes showing a dazzling depth of intelligence and—

Barriers.

"Yes, at the blood lab," he said.

Her gaze returned to the clipboard. "Okay, after each injection, we'll monitor Angie's white blood cells to make certain they don't get too low. If they do, we'll skip one treatment to give her blood levels time to recover, then pick up again the following week."

"I understand." Mark nodded.

"I don't. How come?" Angie asked.

Ever inquisitive, Angie had been on the Internet with Mark last night, reading all they could find out about brain tumors and treatments. She'd even commented that she wanted to be an oncologist like Dr. Shields when she grew up. Mark prayed Angie made it to a very old age.

Emma gazed at Angie with a hint of respect. "That's a very good question. I'm glad you asked. The drugs we're giving you kill the bad cells, but they also kill good cells."

Angie's brow wrinkled. "And we can't let too many good cells die, right?"

Smart kid. Pride surged through Mark. With Angie's intelligence, he was certain she'd make it through med school, if given the chance.

"Right," Emma said.

"But what if the chemo doesn't kill my tumor?"

Mark held his breath, waiting for Emma's response.

Emma's mouth opened and her gaze softened, but she didn't speak right away. She seemed to choose her words carefully. "We have other options. We can use radiation, but we're not to that point, yet. Let's just take it one day at a time, all right?"

Angie smiled and nodded. She looked so trusting as she watched Emma.

Mark's body tensed without him willing it. What if they had to resort to radiation? Brain cells didn't recover from radiation and Angie could lose much of her cognitive ability. What damage would the chemo cause? Her neurosurgeon had told him that once she finished her chemo protocol, she'd have a forty percent chance of never giving birth to her own child. Sometimes he wondered if the treatment was worse than the illness.

Realizing his breathing had quickened and his heart was pounding, Mark tried to calm his troubled mind. One day at a time. Right now, they were fighting for Angie's life.

"Will the chemo make me sick?" Angie asked.

Emma lifted one brow. "I see you have your father's intelligence."

"And her mother's beauty." Mark smiled at Angie and the little girl beamed.

He mentioned Denise for Angie's benefit.

Emma's focus shifted to the alpine picture over his right shoulder and he couldn't help wondering if the mention of Denise bothered her. What a fool he'd been all those years ago to dump Emma for a pretty girl whose father had connections in the business world. Prestige had meant everything to him back then.

"Certain foods react with the drugs we're giving Angie and can create a problem. Do you have the list of things she shouldn't eat?" Emma asked.

"Yeah, we've got it and I'll make sure Angie follows it."

"Okay, pumpkin, you ready?" Sonja came over to the bed, then reached to help Angie sit back.

Lying on the pillow, Angie handed Mark her flowered hat. He noticed Emma's gaze slid over the little girl's bald head where pink scars circled the top right side. Hopefully, her thick hair would eventually grow back and no one would notice.

Emma didn't show even a glimmer of repulsion. Instead a flicker of empathy filled her eyes.

Ah, she's not as indifferent as she wants us to believe.

Sonja lifted Angie's shirt, exposing the porta-catheter installed for administering the chemo injections. The neurosurgeon had warned that, if they didn't use a porta-catheter, by the time Angie turned eighteen, the veins in her arms would collapse. If not handled carefully, the powerful medicine could burn her skin bad enough to require a plastic surgeon to repair the damage. A patch covered the EMLA Cream, which Mark had applied to Angie's skin thirty minutes earlier. Angie shouldn't feel any more than a bit of pressure.

"Is it gonna hurt?" Angie's voice wobbled as she looked at Emma.

Tenderness filled Emma's eyes. "No, sweetie, it shouldn't."

Setting her clipboard aside, Emma slipped her glasses off and tucked them into her pocket before carefully peeling back the Emla patch. She accepted a piece of gauze from Sonja and wiped the white cream off.

"Okay, lie still." Emma's voice soothed.

Mark tensed. Angie clung to his hand, her pulse hammering against her throat.

"Honey, I'm here." He cupped Angie's cheek and looked into her eyes. Bending at the waist, he lowered his face to lean against the pillow. She whimpered and Mark kissed her forehead, speaking calming words to her.

"All done, sweetie," Emma said. "You can sit up now."

Both Angie and Mark breathed with relief. As Emma drew near, he caught her scent, a combination of warm skin and some elusive floral fragrance. Inhaling deeply, he tried to forget why he was here.

"It didn't hurt a bit. Thanks, Dr. Shields." Angie smiled, showing one tooth missing in front.

What a difference. Now the dreaded injection was over, Angie almost seemed her old self again.

"You're welcome." Emma's mouth curled as she disposed of the needle in a box labeled Hazardous Waste.

Placing a small dot bandage over the needle prick, Sonja helped Angie lower her shirt and patted the little girl's shoulder. "You did just fine, kiddo. Do you want to come select a prize from my stash out in the office? I got it special just for your visits."

A grin spread across Angie's face and she nodded.

Sonja took her hand as Angie slid off the bed, then they left the room. Mark picked up Angie's hat and slapped it against his thigh. Emma put her reading glasses on, then picked up her clipboard, jotting more notes.

"Thanks, Emma. I really appreciate this. I can't begin to tell you how much."

"You're welcome. Angie's a great kid." She showed a wistful smile.

A wisp of golden hair slipped free of the tight knot at the back of her neck and curled against her cheek. He longed to reach out and feel the texture of it.

"Yeah, she is." He hesitated, wondering how to say what was on his mind. "Look, Emma, I sense you're uncomfortable with me here. Is it because I was such a dope back in high school?"

Her gaze glanced off his. "I don't know what you mean."

Sure she did. There was no need to pretend. It occurred to him that she was doing her best to hide her injured feelings. Maybe it was a defense mechanism. No, she didn't want him here, but she had put aside her wounded pride to help Angie.

Sudden respect filled him, along with a protective impulse. He shouldn't have reminded her that he had dumped her for Denise all those years earlier. "You've turned out to be an amazing woman, Emmy."

Her eyes widened and she looked startled. "I'm a doctor, Mark. This is what I do."

"Still, I want you to know I'm grateful."

She laughed, a harsh sound with no humor. "Believe me, you'll get my bill."

He chuckled but sensed her deep sarcasm. "Thank

goodness for health insurance. So far, the medical bills are nudging half-a-million dollars, the deductibles large enough to cross my eyes."

After college, he'd worked hard and invested well, but the divorce settlement had drained a large portion of his wealth. He'd been lucky Denise wanted cash and let him buy out her half of the house. To save Angie's life, he'd sell everything he owned and live in a pup tent in the park. Whatever it took. Money didn't mean anything to him now. Not if he lost his daughter.

"You've changed since high school, Mark." Her brows pulled together in a perplexed frown.

Was it that obvious? "Really? How so?"

"You're so gentle with Angie. I remember you being such a jock, laughing all the time, going to parties. I never imagined you'd be such a softy with a little girl of your own."

He remembered, too. All those parties he had attended, and Emma hadn't been invited. He remembered the pain in her eyes when he'd told her he didn't want to go out with her anymore. The slump of dejection in her shoulders and the hurt in her voice when she'd wished him nothing but the best.

Those days had been focused on one thing only. Get the best grades possible, excel at sports and earn a full-ride scholarship to N.Y.U. so he could get a top job making lots of money. What had it mattered that he'd dumped the school bookworm for a hot babe who happened to be the head varsity cheerleader? When he married Denise fresh out of college, he'd been the envy of every other guy at school.

None of that seemed important now. Except for Brett

Anderson, he rarely saw any of his old friends. If only he hadn't been so superficial. But no matter what Denise did or how difficult his life became, he could never regret having Angie.

"That was a long time ago, Emma. Now, I'm a father with responsibilities. When Angie was born, I started thinking about more than just the here and now. I wanted the best for my child, and that caused me to seek a greater power than my own."

Her brows arched. "So, you got religion, huh?"

"You could say that. I'd be lost without God in my life. As I recall, you used to be quite religious yourself."

"Things change."

He ached for her lack of faith. "Sometimes it's hard for me to see my life with eternal eyes, but I came to realize that God has my best interest in mind."

A skeptical frown crinkled her brow and he changed the topic. "When we were in high school, I was just a thoughtless, stupid kid. I hope you'll forgive me for…for everything."

"Of course. There's nothing to forgive." She bit her bottom lip, staring at the brown carpet.

What had her husband's name been?

David.

Although they had divorced, Mark couldn't help envying the man. Emma obviously loved him. Not once in the eleven years they had been married had Mark ever heard Denise say the words, "I love you."

Not even to Angie, and that hurt most of all.

"I know what you mean about things changing." He didn't smile as he spoke. "Life hasn't worked out quite the way I'd planned it."

She blinked, as if digesting this information. "I remember you said you wanted to marry a beautiful socialite and be the CFO of some Fortune 500 company. You wanted to make buckets full of money, go into politics and become president of the United States."

He burst out laughing, thinking how foolish he must have sounded to Emma. Strange that he had never once confided his amitions to Denise. "Not anymore. Now, I'd settle for a quiet evening at home with Angie."

She chuckled, the sound tripping his heart into double-time. "No fancy restaurants?"

"Let's just say I prefer relaxing in my own home."

"Me, too," she conceded.

A long paused followed and Emma tilted her head, seeming to study him. "It seems so strange to see you comforting a little girl. I never envisioned you with so much compassion, Mark."

Ah, that hurt, but he couldn't deny it. "Right now, Angie's most important."

Her brow crinkled with thought. "I'm glad to hear that. If it helps any, I like the new you."

Somehow her words made him want to be even better. For her.

He took a step. "Emma, I hope we can be—"

Angie returned with a Tasmanian Devil sticker planted smack in the middle of her forehead and holding a purple lollipop in her fist.

"Hey, Dad, look what Sonja gave me." She lifted the sucker and pointed at her forehead.

He rubbed her bristly head gently where the new hair growth was starting to come in. It rasped the palm of his hand. "Yeah, that's great. Did you remember to say thank you?"

Angie turned to face Sonja. "Thank you. We get to go for pizza now. Dad said he'd take me to lunch."

"Good for you," Sonja said. "I'd better get back to work."

The nurse slipped out of the room, closing the door behind her. Emma removed her glasses. Heavy lashes fringed her eyes, her skin soft and smooth. If not for the weariness in her gaze, Mark would have thought she hadn't aged a day since high school.

"Just remember, no pepperoni," Emma warned. "It messes with some of the drugs you're taking."

Angie groaned. "But pepperoni's my favorite."

Emma's lips curved into a smile. "Try sausage or Canadian bacon, instead."

"Yuck!" Angie's face contorted. "That's grown-up stuff. Kids like pepperoni."

Emma's lips twitched as she suppressed a laugh. "Okay, just plain cheese. Kids like cheese, don't they?"

"Yeah, that'd be okay, I guess." Angie brightened, but then grouched, "No pepperoni, no raspberries, no peanut butter. How's a kid supposed to live like that?"

Mark chuckled. "Don't be dramatic. I think you'll survive without pepperoni for a year, until we're finished with the chemo."

Emma's gaze slid toward the door. "Well, I've got patients waiting."

"Hey, Dad, can Dr. Shields come to lunch with us?"

Mark lifted his gaze to Emma. Her mouth hung open and she stared at the child with surprise.

He read Emma's body language. Stiff and unyielding, everything about her told him she wanted him to go away and leave her alone. Then she lifted her head and he saw the longing in her eyes, a depth of emotion that told him she wanted him to stay.

She seemed so lost. Maybe they both were.

"Emma, are you——" He swallowed. "Are you free for lunch?"

Mark didn't need any more complications in his life, but he couldn't seem to help himself. It was just lunch. No big deal.

"Thanks, but I can't. I've got to work." Emma choked the doorknob with her hand. "Don't forget to see Darcy at the front counter to set up your next appointment in one week."

And she was gone, just like that. Mark told himself he should be relieved. Instead, he felt empty inside.

Taking Angie's hand, Mark led her out of the examination room and through the long hallway to the front reception counter. Nurses passed back and forth, calling for patients, prepping vials of medicine and IV drips.

Two nurses and three office staff workers stood at the counter, surrounding an elderly Hispanic couple. Mark spoke Spanish fluently and it was difficult not to overhear the conversation. The man and woman sounded upset, their voices escalating until Emma came down the hall to see what the commotion was about.

"What's going on?" Emma asked the receptionist in a disapproving voice.

With just one look, Emma sent most of the office staff scurrying back to their desks. That left Darcy to face the fallout.

"I'm sorry, Dr. Shields, but Mr. and Mrs. Valdez don't speak English, and she seems worried about her treatment," Darcy said.

"Where's Maria?" Emma asked. "She can translate."

"She took some blood samples over to the hospital."

Frustration was apparent on Emma's face. Engrossed in the conversation, Mark didn't notice Angie until too late. The little girl sidled over to Mrs. Valdez, her large eyes filled with sympathy as she reached up and took hold of the woman's hand.

"It's okay," Angie soothed as she stared up at Mrs. Valdez's wrinkled face. "You can use my EMLA Cream, and the needle poke won't hurt a bit."

Angie handed the tube of cream to Mrs. Valdez and Mark's heart turned over. What had he done to deserve this sweet little girl? Truly he had been blessed. Even though she didn't understand what Mrs. Valdez was saying, Angie knew instinctively it was the woman who was sick, not her husband.

"Excuse me, but I speak Spanish," Mark interceded. "Perhaps I can help translate?"

Emma's eyes glowed with relief. "Yes, I would appreciate it. First, tell Mrs. Valdez not to be worried. We only want to help her."

Emma waited patiently while Mark translated for Mrs. Valdez. He could see the earnest concern written on Emma's face and heard the soothing tone of her voice as she explained what Mrs. Valdez could expect from her treatment. Mark's respect for Emma grew as he interpreted questions and responses back and forth. In a matter of minutes, both Mr. and Mrs. Valdez relaxed and smiled. Mark realized then that Emma really did care about her patients, though she seemed to fight it.

"*Gracias.*" The woman nodded at Mark and Emma before she squeezed Angie's hand.

"She's ready," Mark told Emma.

Accompanied by Sonja, the Valdezes shuffled to the treatment room, leaving Mark and Angie with Dr. Shields.

"I didn't know you spoke Spanish, but I'm sure glad you came to my rescue," Emma said.

"Yeah, I took it in college and spent a semester abroad in Spain. It comes in handy for my Hispanic clients."

The tension eased from her shoulders. "Thanks for helping out. I owe you big-time."

He smiled and sank his hands into his pants' pockets. "No problem. I'll collect from you on Tuesday, when I bring Angie in for her next treatment."

Emma glanced at the little girl, a momentary look of panic in her eyes.

"Well, I need to get back to work." Emma headed down the hallway.

"Yeah, thanks again, Emma."

Boy, he was getting mixed signals. Something about Angie bothered her. What could it be? He tried to tell himself Angie's welfare was all that mattered right now. Somehow he wished he dared hope for more.

Chapter Four

Inside her office Emma stared at the closed door after she'd left Mark. Whew, what a rotten situation. If he hadn't been here to translate for her—

Mark had always had a controlling nature. This time it had been a blessing. With Maria out of the office, Emma couldn't deny she was grateful Mark had been here. Perhaps they could schedule Angie's appointment at the same time as Mrs. Valdez's treatment next week. If Maria was away from the office, Mark could translate again.

Emma opened the door and hurried out to the front reception desk before Mark left. She posed the question to him, then waited for his rejection. In high school, he hadn't been interested in helping with fund-raisers or other worthwhile causes. Would he help with this?

"Sure," he agreed readily. "I'd be happy to do it."

His generosity stunned her. Time and fatherhood had really changed him. Maybe his newfound belief in God had also made a difference. He had suffered a divorce, like her, and Emma found herself hoping he didn't lose his child, too. She wouldn't wish that on her worst enemy.

Darcy set the appointment time and Mark left with Angie. Emma stood beside the reception counter for just a moment, remembering Mark's gentleness as Angie received her injection. With aching tenderness, he had held his child close, kissing her, speaking soothing words in her ear.

He seemed so different from the flippant, egotistic boy he used to be. For one insane moment she considered what it might be like to get to know him all over again.

Emma bit her lip, fighting the soft feelings that suddenly overwhelmed her. She'd promised herself she wouldn't get involved with Angie or her father. Yet, here she was remembering every detail of her encounter with them and feeling sentimental about a man she hadn't seen for fifteen years.

Next week, she would let Sonja handle Angie's injection on her own, then pop into the examination room long enough to answer any questions they might have. She was going to put as much distance between herself and Mark Williams as possible.

Renewed confidence steadied her nerves and she went about her business. By four o'clock that afternoon, she had enough time to go into her office and make a few phone calls.

"Sonja, who is Don Yearwood?" she asked, trying to decipher Darcy's hastily scrawled note. "It says he's from the Make-A-Wish Foundation. What does he want?"

"I think he's the director of the Northern Nevada chapter," Sonja supplied. "I'm not sure what he wants. Should I check with Darcy? I think she's still here."

"No, he probably just wants a donation."

Emma dialed the number.

"Hello, Dr. Shields. Thanks for returning my call," Don Yearwood's voice greeted her after she identified herself.

"What can I do for you, Mr. Yearwood?"

"Well, I'll get right to the point, Doctor. Your name has come up on several occasions and you were highly recommended to us by Larry Meacham. He's on the board of directors for our Sacramento California chapter and he thought you might be willing to serve on the advisory committee for the chapter here in Reno."

Larry Meacham again. She couldn't help but feel honored, but the guy was wreaking havoc in her life. First, he sent a pediatric patient to her, now this.

"Oh, I thought you just wanted a donation." Emma's voice sounded wilted.

Don Yearwood's scratchy laugh echoed in her ear. "Well, money is always nice, but we were hoping you might be willing to serve, as well."

It felt like her heart dropped through the floor. Every muscle in her body tightened. If she agreed to his request, she'd be expected to mingle with other people, give of her time and expose herself to other people's sorrows.

Could she do it?

Don cleared his throat. "We're already planning our annual barbecue and frequent flyer mileage fund-raiser for the end of August. We were hoping you might be willing to participate. It's only a few months away. The board's meeting this Thursday evening to discuss more plans. Would you be willing to help?"

Emma twisted the phone cord tight around her

index finger. "Um, what kind of time commitment would it entail?"

"The advisory committee meets once a week, and the fund-raisers and activities are usually scheduled for evenings and weekends. Would that interfere too much with your work schedule and family life?"

She had no family life. Except for her medical practice, she had nothing at all. Not even church. She was too angry at God to worship him.

"No, that schedule should work fine. We can try it out—for a while."

"Great! I'm sure the other members will be delighted. I'll let my secretary know you'll be there."

Don gave her the address and time of the Thursday meeting and she hung up, her hands shaking.

Well, she'd done it now. First Angie, now the Make-A-Wish Foundation. She felt strangely excited by the possibilities. Thursday night, she'd get off work by six o'clock and go somewhere besides her lonely apartment. She'd get to do something besides read medical reports and stare at the television as she ate dinner by herself.

"Well?" Sonja poked her head in the office. "What did Don Yearwood want?"

Emma explained.

"Wow! That's a real honor," Sonja said. "I'm glad they realize what an asset you would be to the committee."

Emma doubted Sonja's words. She felt apprehensive about Mr. Yearwood's invitation.

That night, when she got home, Emma went directly to her bedroom, lifted her son's picture from her dresser and told him all about her day. "I don't know what I would have done with Mrs. Valdez if Mark

Williams hadn't been there to bail me out. And though I'm a bit nervous about the Make-A-Wish thing, I'm also kind of excited to help kids like you. Maybe it's time I got out more."

Yes, it's time.

It was as if someone whispered in her ear. Peace enveloped her and she knew she was doing the right thing. Somehow, she felt more alive than she had since before Brian's death. It was almost as if he were there beside her, urging her to live again, cheering her on.

As she looked at Brian's picture, she didn't feel like crying. Instead, she felt like smiling and sharing. She kissed the glass before putting the picture back on top of her dresser.

Thursday came quicker than Emma expected. The office was a whirl of activity and she had little time to think about her commitment to serve with Make-A-Wish.

That evening, she arrived five minutes early at the brightly lit office on Pyramid Street. They had converted a red-brick home into a business office. The summer sun was still high as Emma parked her green compact car and walked inside the main foyer, which smelled of freshly brewed coffee.

"Dr. Shields? I'm Don Yearwood." A tall, balding man with a bushy mustache held out his hand and Emma took it. "We're glad you could make it. Come on in and help yourself to some juice or coffee. As soon as the others arrive, we'll get started."

He indicated a small conference room with a long table and chairs set all around. Wide windows with open curtains admitted the evening sunshine. To the side of the room sat a counter top with a coffee pot, various cartons of juice, cups, and a plate of fruit, cheese, and doughnuts.

What a combination.

Two men stood at the counter, munching on doughnuts as they talked. On the other side of the room, a man and woman sat at a table, sipping cups of coffee and chatting.

Emma helped herself to some pineapple juice and took a seat at the farthest end of the table, away from everyone else. Setting her notepad on the tabletop, she fidgeted with her pen, unable to deny the prickles of panic dotting her skin. She didn't know what to say to these people. Maybe this was a mistake. It wasn't too late to change her mind.

She stood to leave, but strangers filtered through the doorway and blocked her path.

She sat back down. In the next five minutes, the room filled with people and Don introduced Emma to each one. She pasted a smile on her face as she greeted them. An orthodontist, a lawyer, two bank executives, three small business owners and one housewife who used to be an accountant before she had three young children at home to care for.

An impressive crew.

The meeting was called to order and started with a reading of last week's minutes. Emma was stunned when the door opened and Mark Williams walked in.

What was *he* doing here?

Mr. Yearwood didn't stop his dialogue as Mark surveyed the room, spying an empty chair opposite Emma. Skirting the juice counter, he rounded the table and pulled the chair out, finally spotting her. A smile brighter than a neon light spread across his face and his eyes twinkled as he stared at her.

Emma's throat went dry.

As he sat, he winked at her.

Emma looked away.

"Oh, no," she groaned softly, then covered the sound by taking a hurried sip of juice.

"Mark, since you're the late arrival, how would you feel about coordinating the food and paper goods for the barbecue?" Don asked. "We'll also need you to take a turn manning the hamburger and hot dog booth."

"Sure," Mark agreed. "I've already got the head count. I can pick up the supplies anytime and store them in my garage. I'll get the food the day before the event."

Mark Williams was donating free time to Make-A-Wish? She could hardly believe it.

"Great! Dr. Shields, would you be willing to assist Mark?"

Her mouth dropped open and she answered in a halting tone. "Ooo-kay."

She didn't have a choice. She had committed to help. How would it look if she said no to her first assignment?

Don loosened his tie as he paced in front of the Dry Erase board at the front of the room. "I've contacted Channel 6 News to see if they would include a short broadcast the week before the event asking people to donate their frequent flyer miles to Make-A-Wish. Since it's for a good cause, the news people are willing to do a real nice piece for us. They thought it might be more effective to interview a parent and one of our Wish Kids. Mark, I don't mean to pick on you, but how would you and Angie feel about being interviewed by them?"

Mark sat back, his white shirt stretching taut across his muscular chest. "Let me check with Angie tonight.

I don't think she'll mind. I'll give you a call after I've had a chance to ask her."

"That would be fine."

The meeting proceeded, but Emma heard nothing more. Her ears felt clogged, like she was under water. Breathing deeply, she tried to steady her pounding pulse.

Anxiety attack. That's what her doctor called this crazy, muzzy feeling when she was sure she'd implode. He'd given her pills to take for it, but she was determined to cope without drugs.

Breathe deeply. Everything's okay. You can handle this. Really, you can.

The meeting finally ended and Emma stood on shaky legs, prepared to bolt out of the room.

"Emma!" Mark called to her.

Gritting her teeth, she waited while he rounded the table and came to stand close beside her. Too close.

She took a step back.

"I didn't know you were on the committee, too. When did you join?" he asked.

"This is my first meeting. You could say I was brought in as part of a conspiracy."

One of his brows quirked and he laughed. "Conspiracy, huh? That sounds rather sinister."

When she glanced at Mark and saw amusement playing across his face, she smiled. She couldn't help it. Mark's laughter was infectious and, with a bit of surprise, she found his presence strangely comforting.

"Angie's one of their Wish Kids," he said. "I wanted to be involved, to give back to a wonderful group. I thought I could help make a difference, like so many people have made a difference for Angie and me. I can't begin to thank all the wonderful people who have stepped in and blessed our lives. My business partners, church members, social workers, neighbors."

He moved closer and her eyes widened.

"You," he said.

Staring at the top button on his Oxford shirt, she backed up a step. His gratitude disarmed her. If he only knew what she had done to her own son, he would never want her to doctor Angie.

He stepped closer and she felt cornered. He reached out and put his hand on her arm. Panic lodged in her throat.

"We can wait to pick up the burgers and hot dogs until the day before the barbecue," he said. "Would you be able to go shopping with me for paper plates, napkins and plastic utensils the day after tomorrow?"

"The day after tomorrow?" she repeated in a vague tone.

"Yeah, it's Saturday. You don't have to work, do you?"

She didn't *have* to, but she always did work on the weekend. "No, no, I don't have to work."

She looked at his face. Ah, such nice eyes, crinkling when he smiled. She twined her fingers together, her heels sinking deep in the thick carpet.

He smelled good. Nice and spicy, yet not overpowering.

She stepped back again and her shoulders met the wall with a little thump. She'd forgotten how tall he was.

"I can pick you up," he offered.

She licked her dry lips. "Okay, how about eleven?"

"Good, we can catch some lunch afterward. What's your address?"

Lunch. What was she getting herself into?

As she gave him the information, he scrawled her home address and phone number on a scrap of paper. Folding it, he then tucked it into his front shirt pocket.

Great! So much for keeping her distance. Now he knew where she lived and how to reach her at home.

"How's Angie doing?" She shouldn't have asked, but she really wanted to know. It was her job to ask questions and monitor the girl's progress.

A frown pulled at his brow. "She's as good as can be expected, but she's throwing up and quite weak. I know you said it's normal to feel sick right after a treatment, but I hate to see her like this. That's why I was late tonight. She was sick in the car, so I got it cleaned up and then bought her a sand bucket to carry around when we travel."

"A sand bucket?"

"Yeah, she takes it with her to help prevent accidents. Angie likes it because it has little pink seashells on the rim and it's smaller than the mop bucket."

How ingenious. Pretty sand buckets in the car.

"How's her appetite?" Emma asked.

A labored sigh escaped his lips. "Not good, but Mrs. Perkins tries hard to get her to eat during the day while I'm at work."

"Mrs. Perkins?"

"Our neighbor. She's a widow who watches Angie for me. Usually, she only takes in babies, but Angie isn't up for a busy summer day-care program. She doesn't have that kind of stamina. Instead Mrs. Perkins lets her do puzzles and read, and help tend the babies. Angie can lie down and rest anytime she wants. It's a good, quiet place for her, although Angie tells me the babies cry a lot."

"Ah."

He gave a sad smile. "You know with the brain tumor, all of a sudden, we belong to a club we don't want to belong to. Angie just wants to be a kid. I wish I could give her a normal childhood."

Emma understood. When Brian had become ill, she'd joined that club, too. She opened her mouth to tell Mark about it, but caught herself just in time. "I'm sorry, Mark. I hope we can give you your wish very soon."

He flashed a brilliant smile and her stomach flipped somersaults.

"You've been great, Emma. So many people have helped us. When I got home from work tonight, I found that one of the men from my congregation mowed my lawns this afternoon. His wife brought dinner in and took our dirty clothes to wash. I know those things seem trivial, but it lifted a big burden from me. There are so many good people praying for us."

"That's very kind of them." She could hardly speak around the lump in her throat. She found herself wishing kind members from her congregation had been there when Brian had died, but her husband didn't like structured religion and she'd gone inactive. No one at church had followed up with her to find out why she wasn't attending anymore and she had too much pride to ask for their help during those dark days before and after Brian's death. Would it have made a difference?

The other committee members had left the room, moving toward the main foyer in the outer reception area. The sun had gone down and the wide picture window looked black and vacant.

Just like her heart.

"I was sorry to hear you were divorced," Mark interjected.

Emma froze. Any reminder of her divorce was like meat hooks ripping at her. Guilt rested heavily on her shoulders. Her ex-husband blamed her for the death of their son, and he had been right.

"Yes," she croaked.

"I'm sorry for your loss," Mark said again.

She felt the burn of tears. "Thank you."

"I don't recall your husband. Did I know him?"

Shaking her head, she felt as though a wind tunnel had sucked her up. "No. David and I met in college."

"Ah, and what does he do for a living?"

"While we were married, he owned a construction company. He built things. Usually lush homes with tons of rooms for all my rich medical colleagues."

Resentment filled her tone. She remembered how her husband made contacts with her circle of wealthy doctor friends. For him, her medical degree wasn't about helping save lives, but rather a way to get lucrative building contracts for clinics and homes. Still, Emma couldn't blame him alone for the breakup of their marriage. They'd been struggling for some time before their son's illness. After Brian died, Emma didn't have the heart to try anymore. When David blamed her for Brian's death, the end came swift and sure.

She noticed Mark's contemplative frown. "I'm sorry, I didn't mean to unload or sound so cynical. We divorced about two years ago. It's been really hard, but it wasn't all David's fault—"

Time spun away and she longed to head for the door, but her legs wouldn't move.

"I heard your father died a few years after we graduated from high school," he said. "You've had more than your share of tragedy."

She had been alone long before her father died. They hadn't been on speaking terms and she hadn't known he was gone until after the funeral. He'd been a domineering man who'd made her mother's life miserable. Emma had made up for their lost relationship by showering her love on Brian. Now, she had no one and she couldn't face the pain of losing someone dear ever again.

"I have my practice, and that keeps me busy." Her voice cracked.

He cupped her elbow and squeezed gently, a look of empathy on his face. She wasn't fooling him for a minute. "I get the feeling you miss your husband very much."

She shuddered. "I miss the camaraderie and the close relationship of a husband and wife, but I don't miss the—"

She was telling him too much. She'd almost blurted out that she didn't miss David's accusations or criticism. She no longer loved David, but she missed the warmth of a man nearby when she needed a solid shoulder to lean upon. She missed having someone reach things on the top shelf and be strong for her when she didn't think she could go on alone.

It was too comfortable to confide in Mark. He'd always been easy to talk to.

Another step and he reached his other hand toward her shoulder. Panic overwhelmed her. He was going to hug her. She couldn't allow that—

"Excuse me."

Whirling about, she fled, racing for the door, bumping into Rachel Miller, the accountant housewife with three children.

"Pardon me," she called as she dashed through the foyer and shoved against the glass pane of the outside door.

In the dark parking lot, Emma sprinted for her car, stumbling in her high heels. Even if she broke her leg, she was *not* going to stop until she was in that car.

Turning on the ignition, she jerked the gearshift into reverse and spun out of the parking lot. Looking back in her rearview mirror, she saw Mark standing on the sidewalk, hands in his pants' pockets, staring after her.

Too close. Too close.

She had promised herself she wouldn't become friendly with him. But she'd ended up telling him things she hadn't confided to anyone, not even herself.

Her heart slammed against her chest. She almost ran a red light and the breaks squealed as she forced herself to slow down. She pulled over and stopped the car at the side of the road, trying to calm her nerves before she killed someone—probably herself.

"Oh-hh," she groaned, and leaned her head against the steering wheel.

She brushed angrily at the tears falling down her cheeks. "I don't believe in You, God. You've never been there for me. Why should I believe in You?"

Silence filled her heart. A dark, forbidding void that left her feeling vacant as she stared out her windshield.

Wiping her nose and eyes, she tried to calm her shaking hands and struggled to think of something else. She had two days before Mark came to pick her up to take her shopping. Two days to settle her nerves and gain control.

"I can do this." She clenched her hand and pounded it against the dashboard. "I know I can do this. I won't become emotionally involved with him and I won't let him get close to me ever again."

No matter what, she was *not* going to start to care for him or his sweet little daughter.

Chapter Five

Mark didn't set the alarm on Friday nights. Saturday mornings he slept in, awakened by the sunshine filtering through the shutters in his bedroom. He stretched on the king-sized bed, enjoying some peace after a long, hectic week.

He had needed a good night's sleep. So had Angie.

Today he was going shopping with Emma. The thought of seeing her again made him happy, an emotion he rarely felt these days.

After showering, he pulled on a pair of faded jeans and a blue T-shirt, then went downstairs and found Angie in the family room, watching cartoons.

"Hey, babe, how you doing today?" he asked as he clipped on his wristwatch.

Curled up on the couch with her dogs, she wore her pink fuzzy slippers and lacy jammies. "Fine."

She sounded so grown-up. That was the worst part of this illness. It forced her to lose too much of her innocence.

"How about going to the Pancake House for breakfast?"

Pursing her lips together, she shook her head. "No, thanks. I'm not hungry."

He sat beside her on the couch. Dusty nudged his arm and he petted the fluffy Maltese. "You know that's the chemo talking, right? Remember, we talked about how you need to eat even when you don't feel like it? You have to keep up your strength so your body can fight the tumor."

She tugged at the tassels on the throw pillow. "I know, Dad. But when you just don't feel like eating, it's kind of hard to get any food down."

Laughter rumbled inside him. Her wit amazed him. "Think of it as eating cake or candy. We can douse your pancakes with syrup. You always have room for sweet things, even when you're full, right?"

She made a face. "Not anymore. Even candy doesn't look good to me now."

Which was exactly what worried him. "You have to eat, baby."

Another sigh of disgust. "You're not gonna let it go, are you, Dad?"

"Nope, sorry, hon. I love you too much to ever quit." He rubbed her cheek and she returned his smile.

"Okay, I'll eat, just for you. Let me get dressed." She slid off the couch and headed toward her bedroom.

True to her word, she ate—half a pancake and three gulps of milk. It wasn't much, but at least she consumed something.

On the way to pick up Emma, Angie sat on the front seat of his truck, cuddled next to him. She leaned up to flip on the radio. The Righteous Brothers were singing "You've Lost That Loving Feeling" and Angie sang along. Her voice sounded clear and sweet as bell chimes and he felt a sudden lump form in his throat.

"Okay, we're looking for Poole Avenue," he told her as he peered out the windshield. He switched on his left blinker and changed lanes, skirting around the lazy morning traffic.

"Mommy and Eric used to swim in our pool," Angie said.

He glanced at her. "Oh? Well, it's also the name of the street Dr. Shields lives on. There it is." He pointed at the sign and waited for the light to change colors.

"When did your mom swim with Eric?"

The light changed and Mark pulled out into the intersection, gripping the steering wheel so tight his knuckles whitened.

Angie shrugged. "I don't know. Last time Eric came to the house, before Mom left us. He brought a giant inner tube and Mom giggled and went to get ice for their sodas."

Denise had invited a man over to their house, before the divorce? While their daughter was home and Mark was gone?

Knots of anger coiled inside his stomach. How dare she do such a thing?

He shouldn't be surprised. Denise had always flirted with other men, even after they married. In the beginning, he hadn't cared. He provided her with a lavish lifestyle and Denise looked good on his arm at all the company parties where they wined and dined wealthy clients. But after Angie was born, he found himself wanting more, wanting them to be a devoted and loving family.

He had changed. Denise had not.

It no longer mattered, but Mark couldn't help fuming. Bitterness curled around him like a vine of thorns and he fought off the sick feeling that settled in his gut.

"Um, what were Mom and Eric doing besides drinking sodas?"

"I don't know, just stuff. I wanted to swim, too, but they sent me in to watch TV. Mom laughed a lot, but I didn't think Eric was much fun. He never played with me like you do. He always told me to get lost."

Mark wasn't surprised.

"Dad, I didn't like him," Angie confessed.

He smiled and patted her knee. "That's okay, honey. I don't know him and I don't like him, either."

Mark tightened his jaw. He'd rather shout, but what good would that do—other than frighten Angie and make him feel better? Maybe later that night he'd take a drive alone and scream his head off.

"Fifteen thirty-four. That's the address we need, hon. Can you see it?" He purposefully changed the topic, wanting to feel happier before he got to Emma's house.

"There." Angie pointed at a red-brick duplex with a one-car garage on each side of the structure. Emma's car sat parked out front.

Mark silently admitted he had expected more. Though he suspected she could afford a nice place, maybe a house just wasn't important to Emma.

At the curb, Mark parked the truck. "Let's go in."

Angie slid over as he got out, so he could lift her down. Hand in hand, they walked to the front door and Angie rang the bell.

A birdbath sat in the middle of the well-trimmed

lawn, everything tidy and in its place. Mark expected no less from Emma Shields.

From inside the duplex, Mark heard the sounds of movement and then the door opened and there stood Emma.

At first sight of her, his good mood resumed. She looked ravishing and relaxed in blue jeans and a short-sleeved white shirt, her blond hair loose and curling about her shoulders. As she came near, he caught her scent, some kind of clean fragrance he couldn't quite place. How could plain soap smell so good on a woman?

"I'll be right with you," she said before closing the door again.

Why didn't she invite them in?

"Come on, Angie, let's wait by the truck."

She let go of his hand and sauntered over to the birdbath, smiling at the little sparrows fluttering in the water. As Angie approached, the birds scattered and she giggled. It was good to hear her laugh and to see her taking an interest in life. It helped make up for all the times she was sick.

"Sorry to keep you waiting." Emma came outside and locked the front door.

She wore makeup today, her eyes so blue that a vision of the ocean and a deserted tropical island filled his mind.

Over the years he'd forgotten how beautiful she was. "No problem. Everything okay?"

"Yes." She walked with him to the truck. "I had to finish some reports and they took longer than I planned."

"Do you ever stop working?"

She shot him a look. "Do you?"

He laughed. "Touché. But I've heard that most

things get done by busy people who are tired and don't have time."

Inclining her head toward Angie, she met his gaze. "You've had more than your fair share of things to handle. You're doing a marvelous job with her."

Her praise warmed his heart. "Thank you."

Angie waited as Mark opened the door and held out a hand to assist her and Emma up into the high cab. He closed the door, then went around to the driver's seat and got in.

"So, how much stuff do we need to buy?" Emma asked.

"A *lot.*" He chuckled. "That's why I brought the truck. I figure my garage is going to be overflowing before this barbecue is over with."

"It's for a good cause." She looked at Angie. "Have you made a wish yet, with Make-A-Wish?"

"Yeah, Dad and I are gonna go to Disney World for Christmas. It's all I could think of. They couldn't give me what I really wished for."

"Oh, and what's that?" Emma asked.

Angie shrugged. "A mom."

Mark noticed Emma had turned to look out the window, her gaze wistful. Suddenly the happy moment evaporated, replaced by an uncomfortable silence.

They didn't speak much as they drove to a warehouse where they could buy bulk items. Parking as close to the entrance as possible, Mark leaned against his door. "Wow, look at all the cars. It's going to be a zoo in there."

Emma smiled. "Saturday shopping always is. Too many busy people with errands."

"Like us." He grinned. "Well, let's get to it."

He got out and went around to open Emma's door, but

she beat him to it and slipped out of the truck without his help. She grasped Angie around the waist, lifting her down.

"Thanks," Angie said.

"You're welcome, sweetie."

Sweetie. Mark loved it when Emma loosened up like this.

As they neared the warehouse, Angie walked between Mark and Emma. His daughter reached up and clasped his hand. When she also took Emma's hand, Mark blinked.

At first Emma's eyebrows shot up and her lips parted with surprise. Then she accepted Angie's contact and even seemed to enjoy it.

"Swing me, you guys. Swing me!" Angie ordered as she pumped their arms back and forth.

Mark was amazed Angie had the energy to swing. It delighted him, although he didn't think it wise.

"No, honey. I don't want to jar you around," he said.

"Ah." She groaned. "It won't hurt me."

"I just want to be sure. You've got a lot of stuff going on inside your head right now, and I think we should keep you calm. Don't you agree, Emma?"

"Well, I don't think it would hurt her, but that's up to you."

Angie showed a toothless grin and Mark couldn't resist laughing. "Okay, I can't fight both of you."

In unison, Mark and Emma swooped the child forward and back, forward and back. Angie's giggles rang throughout the parking lot and, by the time they reached the front of the store, they were all breathless with laughter.

Emma and Mark each took a shopping cart and

entered the warehouse. Angie wasn't strong enough to walk around the store for very long.

"Do you mind pushing her?" he asked Emma. "I can push the heavier cart."

"Of course," Emma agreed.

Row by row, they collected heavy-duty paper plates, utensils, napkins and cups. Both carts were overflowing by the time they made it to the checkout line, and Mark lifted Angie out and placed her on her feet. He paid the bill, then stuffed the receipt into his pocket.

"Hey, can we get a hot dog?" Angie asked when she saw the refreshment stand.

Mark waggled his eyebrows at Angie. "I'll bet we could get you some fruit to eat."

"But I want a hot dog," she insisted.

He frowned. "What do you think, Dr. Shields?"

"Actually, at this point, calories are as important to Angie as nutrition is. If she'll eat a hot dog and a chocolate shake, let her have it, Mark. She's losing too much weight."

"Okay, Angie, the doctor has spoken. A hot dog it is."

"Hooray!" Angie cheered and squeezed Emma's hand. "I'm glad you're here, Dr. Shields."

Mark felt grateful Angie was interested in eating anything. He left them and the carts to go purchase hot dogs, fruit cups and drinks. Instead of a chocolate shake, he compromised by buying Angie a fruit smoothie but was disappointed when she drank only a quarter of it. He finished off the rest while Angie went to get more napkins and ketchup.

He kept a close eye on her as she darted through the crowd of diners. "It seems I keep finishing off the food

Angie doesn't eat. At this rate, Angie's going to get skinnier and I'm going to get a big gut."

Emma's eyes glimmered and she laughed, the sound soothing to his soul. "I highly doubt that. Do you still go jogging every day?"

He shook his head. "Nah, I haven't done that for about a year. There just isn't enough time anymore."

"Well, I guess there are times when you're just too busy to do everything you want. I'm sure it's a big sacrifice caring for Angie by yourself."

"Not at all. It's no sacrifice when you love your child. I'd give my life for Angie."

Biting into her hot dog, Emma chewed thoughtfully and swallowed before speaking. "Yes, I understand that feeling."

"You do?"

She looked away, her eyes filled with sadness. If he didn't know better, he would guess she spoke from experience. But how could she?

"Did you ever make it to the Olympics?" she asked. "I know you were training for it in high school. Coach Allen said you were good enough."

Mark tensed. She'd hit a raw spot and he took a deep, settling breath.

Chapter Six

"No, I never made it to the Olympics," Mark answered Emma's question. "I was on the track team in college, but Denise didn't like it. After we got married, work and family got in the way—not that I regret it."

Emma understood that feeling. Brian and David had been her life, torn from her in the blink of an eye. What she wouldn't give to have her family back.

She tried not to think about that, enjoying Mark's company instead. It had been a long time since she'd gone shopping with someone. And this was the best hot dog she'd eaten in years.

"What about you?" Mark asked. "Did you ever go to Nigeria after medical school? I remember you used to talk about becoming a doctor and taking off a year to help the sick people in Africa."

She burst out laughing. "We made such plans, didn't we?"

"Why didn't you go?" He tilted his head to one side.

Emma stilled. "As you say, life got in the way. After

the divorce, I didn't feel like doing anything. So I threw myself into my work."

"To forget?" he asked.

"To live. Even a doctor has bills to pay."

"I'm sorry, Emma. It must have been difficult for you."

She lifted one shoulder in a shrug. "It was, but you of all people understand. You're going through the same kind of thing."

"But I've still got Angie."

He showed a tender smile, his laughing eyes almost green in this lighting. The buzz of cash registers and chatter filled the air, along with the scent of cooking hamburgers. She couldn't look away, captivated by the depth of longing she saw on his face. So many words were spoken in those silent moments. The understanding of what it was to fight for someone you loved. Time stood still and Emma's pulse quickened, her breathing became shallow.

He leaned his elbows on the table. "When we were in high school, you were always the one who believed in God. What happened?"

"I had no reason to believe anymore."

"That's rather cynical, don't you think?"

She squeezed her hot dog. "This world is cold and heartless, and only the strong survive."

"That's your hurt talking."

She snorted. "How can you know for sure that there is a God? Nothing makes sense to me anymore."

He paused as he considered her words.

"I know you've been hurt, Emmy, but look at all the good things in your life."

Clasping her hands together, she refused to meet his eyes. She looked across the crowd of people thronging the store, anxious until she saw Angie's head bobbing about as she stood on tippy-toe to reach the napkin dispenser. "What if you're wrong, Mark? What if there isn't anything else?"

Part of her wanted Mark to agree with her and part of her wanted him to convince her she was wrong. In many ways, she felt like a rebellious teenager, daring God to prove He really existed.

"Without God and the Atonement of Jesus Christ, our lives would be absolutely hopeless, Emma. I *know.*" His words were so intense that she paused.

"I wish I had your conviction."

"I know God led me to you, to heal Angie. I can't tell you how many hours I've spent on my knees praying for help, and then we found you. I don't believe it was just by chance."

Her mouth went dry and tears of frustration burned her eyes. She'd never been the answer to anyone's prayer before. At least, not that she was aware of. "Don't say that, Mark. What if I let you down?"

"You won't. Let's just trust our Heavenly Father. He'll help us do what's right for Angie."

She hadn't put faith in God since Brian's death and she had no reason to start trusting Him now. Yet, Mark made it sound like they were a team, planning a strategy to beat the evil tumor. Somehow it felt good to be included. To have someone need her so badly. And yet—

What if he lost Angie? Would he blame Emma and doubt God then?

"I hope you always feel that way, Mark. I hope you never lose your faith, no matter what comes along."

He reached across the table and covered her hand

with his and gave it a squeeze. His eyes were mesmerizing. "I won't. No matter what."

She stared into Mark's eyes.

"Emmy?"

"Yes?"

"You have ketchup on your face."

She blinked as he wiped her chin with his finger and a smile widened his handsome mouth.

"Oh." Pulling a tissue from her purse, she scrubbed her chin, embarrassed.

She felt like a young schoolgirl again, not a mature professional doctor discussing theology with a man she'd had deep feelings for at one time in her life.

Angie broke the moment when she returned with the napkins. Dropping them beside Emma's paper plate, she sidled next to Mark on the bench. She leaned her head down as she stared at a splotch of grime on the tabletop.

"Come here, hon. That doesn't look too sanitary." He tucked her against him, resting her head against his side as he rubbed her back.

Mark was extremely protective of Angie, yet so gentle. Emma couldn't really blame him, though there were times when he probably shielded her too much. No doubt fear of losing his child was the reason why.

"Are you tired out?" He tugged on the brim of Angie's baseball cap and kissed her forehead.

"Yeah, I don't feel good. Can we go, Dad? People are staring at me."

Emma looked up, noticing several people watched Angie, their eyes filled with sympathy. Even with the hat, it was easy to see Angie's bald head and know she was sick, but the attention bothered the little girl. Emma remembered how people stared at Brian, his gaunt face and haunted, vacant eyes.

Mark scowled and the people averted their gazes.

"Sure, babe." He smiled at Emma. "You ready to go, Dr. Shields?"

"Yep."

Without warning, Angie threw up. With a cry of disgust, people scurried to get away from their table. Emma found herself cradling Angie as Mark raced for more napkins.

"I forgot my sand bucket," Angie cried, her nose dripping as tears ran down her pale face.

"Shh," Emma soothed, and pressed napkins into Angie's hands, then rubbed the girl's back in comforting circles. "No harm done. It'll be all right."

Angie clutched Emma's arm and whispered wretchedly. "Everyone's staring."

"It doesn't matter. Here comes your dad. We'll get out of here soon. Here, let me."

Emma took the napkins from Mark and wiped Angie's face.

"Everything okay?" Mark asked in an anxious tone as he tossed a wad of paper towels onto the table to cover the mess.

Emma's heart went out to him. He was trying hard to be upbeat for Angie's benefit, but Emma could tell how harried he felt.

"Sure, everything's fine," Emma tried to reassure him. She turned Angie over to his care, then began to clean up the table.

"Emma, you don't need to do that. I'll take care of it as soon as I get Angie comfortable." Mark tossed an embarrassed look in her direction.

"It's okay, Mark. I don't mind."

By this time, an employee of the store headed toward them carrying a bucket of sudsy water. With a half smile and a word of apology, Emma turned the chore over to the janitor.

With some semblance of order returned, Mark picked up Angie in one arm and wheeled his cart outside. Emma followed, grateful to leave the place. Angie clung to her father, leaning her head against his neck, her eyes closed. His biceps bulged as he balanced the little girl and pushed one of the carts with his free hand.

"Do you want me to stay here with Angie while you take the carts out to the truck? I don't mind waiting with her," Emma offered.

"Nah, I can carry Angie and push a cart at the same time. I'm Super Dad." He kissed Angie on the cheek. She showed a wan smile, but not much else. No doubt, she was ready for a long nap.

Together, Mark and Emma made their way out to his black Silverado truck. After securing Angie inside the cab with her sand bucket in her lap, Mark climbed up on the tailgate and accepted the boxes of plates and cups Emma tossed to him.

"Thanks for your help back there," he said.

"No problem. I'm sure it's just the chemo causing her stomach to be upset. It'll soon pass."

"We make a good team," he observed.

She wasn't going to respond to that.

"How did they rope you into serving on the advisory committee for Make-A-Wish?" Mark asked.

"I got a call out of the blue one day. Larry Meacham

is an old med school friend and he suggested my name to the board of directors."

Mark laughed. "What a coincidence. Larry's our neurosurgeon at U.C.S.F. When I mentioned to Sonja that I was involved in Make-A-Wish, she suggested you might like to work with them, too."

Emma's eyebrows shot up in surprise. "Sonja suggested it?"

"Yep." He grunted as he pushed all the packages to the front of the truck bed.

Sonja? Doing a little matchmaking with Larry Meacham? The two knew each other, so it was possible. Or was Sonja just trying to get Emma out of her safe little cocoon? Emma needed to have a chat with her interfering nurse.

Mark climbed down from the truck bed and closed the tailgate. He dusted off his hands and smiled at Emma.

"I've got some questions for you," he said.

"Oh?" Emma held her breath.

"First, what can I do to get Angie to eat a little more and keep it down? She's getting really thin. She only weighs forty-two pounds and you saw what happened after she ate her lunch."

Emma sighed. "Yes, I've noticed she's losing too much weight. If she gets down to forty pounds, we'll have to start feeding her intravenously."

Mark grimaced, his voice low enough that Angie couldn't hear. "Can't we do something else? It's killing me to watch her waste away like this."

Emma understood too well. She'd lost count of the sleepless nights she'd fretted over Brian for this very same scenario. It was horrible to watch your child slowly die.

"I'll write you out a prescription for an appetite enhancer."

"That would be great."

"Mark, there are some wonderful advances in medicine that can benefit Angie. If you have a concern, just ask and we'll figure something out."

"I will. Thanks, Doc."

"And what was your other question?"

"Well, I was just wondering if you—if you'd like to have dinner with Angie and me Monday night. Brett and Tina Anderson will be in town. I thought it might be fun for us all to get together and reminisce about old times."

Emma felt a rush of excitement. She hadn't seen Brett and Tina in years. They had been such good friends in high school, double-dating with Emma and Mark. Back then, they had joked that they would be married and they'd all live on the same street in the same town and be friends forever.

Brett and Tina had married, but Emma got the boot.

"You still keep in touch with them?" she asked.

"Yeah." He shifted his weight. "They're the only ones I keep regular contact with. Brett was there for me when Denise left. Since we all have a lot in common, I thought you might want to come spend the evening with us."

Was this a date?

"Uh, I'm not sure," she said.

Run! Get out of here, now. Don't let him get too close.

"Believe it or not, I make a mean pot roast," he urged. "It's my mother's old recipe. Even Angie likes it."

He folded his arms across his chest. Her gaze followed the motion and she noticed a bead of perspiration in the hollow of his throat. She was still woman enough to appreciate a handsome man, but no. She couldn't have dinner with him. She'd gotten too close already. "I'm sorry, but I can't."

His eyes narrowed. "Can't or won't?"

Her cheeks heated. "I think it would be better if I pass. I don't date my patients, or their fathers. Thanks anyway."

He looked startled.

"Date? Oh, well, I didn't think of it like that, uh—never mind." He smiled, but it didn't reach his eyes.

It wasn't a date. Then what was it?

"Are you talking just friends getting together?" she asked.

A half smile curved his handsome mouth. "Well, yeah. Something like that. Old friends having dinner and catching up on each other's lives."

The idea had appeal. She liked being with Mark and Angie and couldn't prevent feeling delighted by his invitation. She would love to see Tina and Brett after all these years.

"I just wanted to say thank you for everything you've done to help Angie and me." Mark held his hands up. "No pressure on any of us. Just food and good conversation."

"Oh, well, in that case, I accept."

"You do?" He blinked.

"Yes, if I can bring something."

A wide smile spread across his face. "Okay, how about bringing a salad?"

"You got it. What time and where?"

Something deep inside warned that she'd be better

off to refuse and stay home alone. But somehow, safe and lonely no longer held any appeal. For the first time in months, she'd have dinner with old friends and muse about happier times.

She hoped she didn't come to regret accepting Mark's offer.

Chapter Seven

"So, your mom and dad are divorced, huh?" Carla Perkins asked Angie as they sat together in front of the TV at Mrs. Perkins's house.

"Yeah, they're divorced." Angie hated talking about her mom and dad breaking up, but she didn't want to make Carla angry by telling her so. Angie's dad was at work and the little girls were playing a video game together.

Three years older than Angie, Carla was Mrs. Perkins's granddaughter, visiting from Nebraska. With her pierced ears and long, brown hair tied in a thick braid down her back, she seemed quite wise and worldly to Angie. Plus, it was fun to have an older kid to play with for a change. The babies Mrs. Perkins took care of were cute, but they cried a lot and got on Angie's nerves sometimes. And Carla didn't run away, fearing Angie was "diseased."

Carla huffed. "My mom and dad are divorced, too."

Concentrating on the game, Angie pressed her tongue against the roof of her mouth as their cars raced down the pretend track on the television screen. She worked on making her car dodge obstacles that magically appeared in her path as she tried to reach the finish line before Carla's car.

"Really?" Angie asked.

"Yep." Carla also stared at the screen. "But then my mom started dating again, and now she's remarried."

"Do you live with your dad?"

"Nope. I'm with my mom most of the time. But I spend Christmas and six weeks every summer with my dad. I like coming to Reno because I get to see my grandma."

"I live with my dad." It was nice to find another kid like her. Most of the kids at church didn't have divorced parents.

"When's he gonna get remarried?" Carla asked.

"I don't know." Angie forced her gaze to remain on the screen.

"Is he dating anyone, yet?"

Angie glanced at Carla. "No. But I think my mom will come home soon."

"Pow! Game over." Carla burst out laughing as she drove Angie's car off the side of the road.

"Hey, no fair. Let's go again."

"Okay," Carla agreed.

"Hey, you two," Mrs. Perkins called from the doorway. "Lunch in five minutes."

"What is it today?" Carla called without looking up.

"Chicken strips, string beans, apple slices and cheese sticks."

"Yum! Chicken strips. My favorite." Carla licked her lips with delight.

Angie remained silent. Macaroni and cheese was her favorite, but even that didn't tempt her anymore. Since she got sick, she didn't even like chocolate-chip ice cream much and she hated the taste of toothpaste. Dad said it was because of the chemo. *Everything* was because of the chemo.

Mrs. Perkins went back into the kitchen and Carla blurted, "You know your mom's not coming back, right? They never do."

Angie frowned, not liking the sound of that. "But you live with your mom and see her all the time."

Carla shrugged. "Yeah, but we moved to Nebraska and she flies me here to visit Dad. After a while, she got remarried, and so did my dad. Now, my new stepmom's gonna have a baby pretty soon."

Angie's mouth dropped open. "A baby? You mean, like all the babies here in your grandma's house?"

Carla took that opportunity to surge her car ahead of Angie's. It was no use. Carla had a lot more practice at playing this video game.

"Of course, silly. What kind of baby did you think I meant? It won't be like a puppy or a kitty, and this baby won't belong to other people. It'll be all mine."

Now that idea appealed to Angie. A little brother all her very own. He wouldn't ever leave her and he wouldn't ever cry because she'd take good care of him and make him happy.

"Wham! I got you again." Carla whooped with glee.

Angie dropped her game control and scooted away to rest her back against the edge of the couch. She didn't care that Carla was better at Crash Car Racers. Right now, she wanted to know more about how to get a baby brother and a new mommy.

"I've always wanted a little brother," Angie confided.

"You know your dad has to get married first, right?"

No, she hadn't really thought about that, but she wasn't about to confess it to someone as grown up as Carla. "Sure, I know that."

Carla rolled onto the carpet, lying on her stomach as she propped her chin on her hands. "So, who have you got lined up as a potential mom?"

"I want my old mom back."

"Look, divorced people don't get back together," Carla lectured. "They just date other people. Your mom left you, so move on."

"But what if my dad gets remarried and my new mom moves on, too?" The thought terrorized Angie. Did all moms leave, or just hers and Carla's?

Carla hunched her shoulders. "It happens sometimes, but your dad's never left you, right?"

Angie shook her head. "No, Daddy would never leave me."

"You want a mom, don't you?" Carla pressed.

Angie's eyes widened and she nodded her head. "Yeah, but I don't want a mom who'll hurt Dad and leave us again."

"Then you'll have to scout out potential women for your dad to date, and choose carefully."

More than anything else in the world, Angie wanted a mom to help Daddy be happy again. Since the divorce, Dad still smiled and teased her, but he wasn't the same anymore. He seemed miserable deep inside and she didn't know how to change that. Maybe a new wife was the answer.

"Your best bet is to tell your dad who you like the most," Carla advised.

"You think that would really work?"

"Sure! Dads care if you like who they're dating. Just don't be pushy. Give them some space when they're together, or he'll catch on to what you're doing and break up with the mom you want. It helps if she's kind of pretty. Then, you just sit back and let him do the work and you'll have a new family again." Carla clicked her fingers together, as if it were a magic trick.

"Girls, come and eat," Mrs. Perkins called.

Carla bounded to her feet and scampered toward the kitchen. "Come on, Angie. I'm hungry."

Angie was slow to follow. She was still thinking about what Carla said. She hadn't liked it when Mom brought Eric over to the house when Daddy was at work, but now Mom was gone, so why shouldn't Daddy marry someone else?

Her heart yanked inside her chest. Why didn't Mommy call? Was she still embarrassed by Angie because she had no hair anymore? Maybe Mommy was too busy with Eric and she didn't have time for a kid with a brain tumor.

As she followed Carla into the kitchen, she remembered waking up in the middle of the night once to use the bathroom. As she'd walked down the hall, she'd heard Daddy in his bedroom crying. When she peeked around his door, she saw him on his knees, praying. She'd never seen him cry like that before. He never seemed bothered because Angie had lost all her hair, so that couldn't be why he was upset. She thought he missed Mommy. Now she wondered if he just felt bad because he was lonely and wanted another lady to take Mommy's place.

She pulled her chair back from the table and slid onto her seat, catching the scent of crispy chicken tenders fresh from the oven. Normally she loved to eat them. Right now, her stomach churned and she stared at the food Mrs. Perkins scooped onto her plate. She’d rather lie down on the couch for a while.

“There, sweetheart.” Mrs. Perkins beamed a smile as she poured Angie a tall glass of milk. “A nice, balanced meal. And I’vc got vanilla ice cream with chocolate syrup for dessert.”

“Hooray!” Carla cheered.

The girls folded their arms as Mrs. Perkins offered a blessing on the food. Then, Angie watched Carla eat.

Daddy deserved to have a good woman to love him, but who would be willing to raise a sick kid?

Yes, Angie definitely should think more about getting a new mom. Maybe she should look over the ladies in church on Sunday.

Chapter Eight

Sunday morning Dad led Angie into the main entrance of the church. Dad looked handsome in a dark suit, white shirt and tie. Before they'd left the house, she'd made sure he splashed on some aftershave. He'd smiled and kissed her nose as she straightened his collar and smoothed his hair.

While she waited inside the foyer for Dad to take care of some church business, she tilted her head to see who was there. Two girls from Angie's Sunday school class walked by, but Angie didn't say hello. Besides, they called her "baldy" all the time. She smiled when they hurried away. Only the grown-up women interested her today. Maybe someone here might like to marry Daddy.

Hannah Nesbitt waddled down the hall wearing a Hawaiian skirt with large orange flowers. She wasn't married and Angie could tell she liked Dad. A lot.

When Hannah saw him, her face lit up and she pushed her way over to greet him.

"Good morning." She shook Dad's hand hard and smiled big.

"Hello, Miss Nesbitt. How are you today?" Dad asked.

The odor of foot cream settled over Angie and she crinkled her nose. Dad sometimes used it when he had athlete's foot, but Angie could tell the smell came from Hannah.

"Oh, I'm fine," Hannah squeaked in her nasal voice.

Dad stepped back and cleared his throat, but Hannah didn't let go of his hand. His face flushed a deep red and Angie could tell he felt uncomfortable.

"Well, almost time to go in." He dragged his hand free and directed Angie into the chapel.

Angie breathed with relief. Hannah was nice, but somehow Angie knew Dad wouldn't want to marry her. Angie didn't want her for a mommy, either. She didn't seem the right type to bake cookies, take her to the park or read her stories.

Organ music sifted over the air, a soft hymn that made Angie feel warm inside. She could see Mrs. Hampton sitting up at the organ, her eyes focused on the keys as she played the music. It'd be nice to have a mom who could teach her piano, but Mrs. Hampton had a husband.

Mrs. Johnson stood beside the door to the chapel and she smiled as she handed Dad a program. Then she bent over and pinched Angie's cheek. "Well, hello, Angie. How are you feeling, dear?"

Ouch! Angie hated it when Mrs. Johnson did that. Angie rubbed her stinging cheek and sidled closer to Dad. He put his hand on her shoulder, both in sympathy and as a warning not to be rude. "Fine, thanks."

Mrs. Johnson's husband died last year. She had to be at least forty five. Way too old for Dad.

Dr. Shields came to mind. Dad laughed a lot when

he was around her. Angie could tell from the way he leaned close to Dr. Shields that he liked her lots. She needed a family, too. If only he would fall in love with Dr. Shields. Dad would be happy again and Angie would have a new mom and possibly a baby brother. Everyone would win.

When Dad led Angie up the aisle, she tugged on his hand. “No, let’s sit back here today, Dad.”

He hesitated. “In the back row? Why?”

“‘Cause I want to see everyone.”

He frowned as she pulled him over to the back pew and plopped down on the cushioned seat.

“Why do you want to see everyone?” he asked.

“Oh, just ‘cause.”

Good thing he didn’t ask more questions. Carla told her not to be too obvious when she picked out a mommy, but it was kind of hard.

He settled back against the bench and opened his suit coat to let her cuddle in against his side and wrap the coat around her. Angie loved the warmth and she could check his pocket for candy or gum. He never minded, unless she rattled the wrapper too loudly.

People milled around as they looked for a place to sit. Three boys older than Angie laid out hymnals and some moms took their kids to the restroom or for a last drink of water before the service began. The low hum of music and chatter filtered around as Angie surveyed the room.

A pretty woman with dark hair appeared at the doorway. Angie didn’t remember her name because she didn’t come to church often. She sat up straighter when the woman walked past wearing one of those frilly white silk blouses Mom liked, except Angie could see the lady's black bra underneath. Angie glanced at Dad to catch his expression. His eyes widened and his ears reddened before he looked away.

Angie sighed and sat back, disappointed.

Several more women filed by. Those who had a man with them, Angie ignored. One wore a dress with a neckline so low that Angie saw lots of skin.

Dad's ears got redder.

Another lady walked past and Angie coughed at her heavy perfume smell. Dad didn't like it, either. He blinked his eyes as if they stung. When Angie waved a hand in front of her nose, he glanced at her but didn't say anything.

Again, Dr. Shields came to mind, with her pretty eyes, soft hands and pleasant smile. Daddy had invited Dr. Shields over for dinner with Brett and Tina tomorrow night, so he must like her. And she was a doctor who never seemed embarrassed to be around a sick kid without hair.

And then, Angie saw her. A new woman sitting up front next to Mrs. Newmann, kind of pretty, and just about Dad's age. The lady had to be a visitor. Maybe she was Mrs. Newmann's daughter or something. Angie waited to see if she had a man with her. No one showed up and Angie started to get excited.

She glanced up at the pulpit as the men assembled. The service was about to start. She had to act fast.

Hopping off the bench, Angie hurried up the aisle to speak to the visitor.

"Angie," Dad called, but she kept going.

A man stood and a hush settled over the congregation. Angie leaned close to the new woman, whispering quietly. The woman shook her head and Mark sat forward, prepared to go and retrieve his wayward daughter. Just then, she hurried back to him and the new lady tossed him a look of astonishment before she turned to speak to Mrs. Newmann.

What was going on?

Mark frowned at Angie as she took her seat and the service began. He leaned close and spoke against her ear. "What were you doing, kiddo?"

"Oh, nothing important."

Nothing important? The two women had their heads close together, whispering. Simultaneously they turned and stared at him. When Mrs. Newmann shook a finger at him, he squirmed in his seat.

"Angie, what did you say to her?" he asked more insistently.

"I asked, but she's already married. She's Mrs. Newmann's daughter visiting from Vegas," she whispered back.

Mark groaned. No wonder the two women were looking at him with a mixture of pity and amusement.

Sighing deeply, he slumped in his seat, wishing he could disappear. Angie was matchmaking. Scoping out the women like she would choose a puppy in a pet store. Now, Mrs. Newmann thought *he* had put Angie up to asking if her daughter was married. He could imagine the field day the gossips would have with that tidbit of information.

"Angie, I don't want you to—"

At that precise moment Hannah Nesbitt thumped through the Chapel doors and hurried up the aisle to take her seat. Mark stared after her, unable to believe his eyes. She had obviously just come from the restroom. The back of her flowered skirt was accidentally stuck up in the top of her waistband.

Mark blinked. He'd never seen panties that shade of hot pink before.

Mrs. Johnson caught Hannah before she sat down and tugged her skirt out of the waistband. Hannah squealed and blushed a color equal to her underwear before she plopped down and buried her head in a hymnal.

Compassion filled Mark for her embarrassment, but he couldn't suppress an inward laugh. What a day this was turning out to be.

He looked at Angie and found her gaping at Hannah, her eyes wide as saucers. He gave his daughter a slow, stern shake of his head and mouthed the words, "Noo waay."

Angie heaved a sigh of disappointment and stared at the floor as she scuffed the toe of her shoe against the green carpet. She looked defeated. Until that moment, Mark hadn't realized how much she missed her mother.

He thought about Emma Shields. She smelled like flowers and had a soothing laugh that made him feel warm and happy inside. He remembered how she'd rubbed Angie's back and wiped her face with a napkin when she threw up yesterday. She instinctively knew what Angie needed and, in spite of her barriers, showed compassion for his daughter he found strangely comforting and disarming.

Mark's gaze wandered around the women sitting in the congregation. Not one of them met his standards.

Either they were married, too old and stuffy, or too eager. Any woman that married him would be taking on a lot of responsibility with a sick child. No doubt it was best he remain single, at least until Angie's illness stabilized.

For the rest of the service, Mark tried to focus on the sermon about the virtuous woman in Proverbs being a crown unto her husband.

"In Proverbs 3:5, it says, 'Trust in the Lord with all thine heart; and lean not unto thine own understanding.'"

Mrs. Newmann tossed Mark a reproachful look. Great. Word would soon spread throughout the congregation that he was on the hunt for a new wife.

By the end of Sunday school, Angie looked tired, from the chemo or all her matchmaking efforts, he wasn't sure. Either way, he didn't have the heart to scold her when they got home.

He fed her as much mac and cheese as he could coerce her to eat, then put her down for a nap. Alone in the family room, he opened his Bible to Proverbs. He sat before the fireplace and started to read, thinking about what he really wanted in a wife and mother for Angie.

Emma came to mind and he set the scriptures aside, letting the thought of her fill him with warmth. She'd be coming to dinner tomorrow night and he'd get the chance to see her again. He couldn't explain the elation that overcame him. Maybe he ought to think about asking her out on a real date.

He shook his head. "Emma deserves better than a man like me, Lord. I sure messed things up with Denise."

All things are made possible to him that believeth.

He did believe. Truly, he did. But Angie was sick and

his divorce hadn't been final that long. He could be on the rebound, and it wouldn't be fair to Emma or Angie to get involved with another woman so soon.

Sitting back in the easy chair, he stared at the ceiling fan as it went 'round and 'round.

Maybe he'd never get a second chance.

Chapter Nine

This was not a date. It wasn't.

Mark picked up a bottle of aftershave and splashed some onto his palm. As he patted it onto his clean-shaven face, he winced at the sting.

No, not a date. Just a thank-you dinner for Emma and a get-together with old school chums. After all these years, he was looking forward to sharing lots of laughter and memories with Brett, Tina and Emma.

He glanced at the clock radio sitting next to his bed. His guests would be arriving soon and he wasn't ready. What had possessed him to invite Emma over to his home? He must be insane to even consider such a thing. If only he weren't so nervous, like he was going on his first date.

Thank goodness Angie, Brett and Tina would be here. With his six-year-old hovering close by, he doubted Emma would get the wrong impression. He just wanted to express his gratitude and friendship, nothing more.

Yeah, sure.

A niggling voice spoke the truth inside his head even when he didn't want to believe it. He couldn't deny his attraction to Emma, but right now wasn't the time to think about romance. He'd keep this strictly platonic. No emotions, no sentiment. Just a pleasant evening. He sure needed it.

"Wow, Dad, you look great. I'll bet Dr. Shields will be impressed." Angie came into his room and plopped belly-first onto his bed. She wore shorts, a T-shirt, sandals and a Giants baseball cap.

The mattress bounced as she propped her chin on her hands, her elbows digging into the downy comforter.

"You think so?" He tucked the bottom of his white polo shirt into the top of his gray slacks.

"Definitely. Women like a man who smells good, too."

He threaded his belt through the loops, then fastened it before he sat in the chair beside the window and pulled on his socks. "Now, how do you know that?"

"Us girls know these kinds of things, Dad."

He chuckled as he tied his shoes. "You're growing up way to fast for me, babe."

He stood and went to the dresser where he snapped on his watch. Where did Angie get her ideas? Sometimes she was too smart for her own good.

"Dad?"

"Hmm?"

"Carla says Mommy's not coming back. She says Mommy doesn't want us anymore. Is that true?"

Regret riddled him. Yes, it was true. But how could he say something like that to his sweet daughter? As she got older, Angie would arrive at her own deductions. He didn't want to be guilty of souring her toward her mother.

"Not entirely, honey. Mom won't be coming back to live with us, but she loves you and you'll see her again for visits."

He hoped his words were true.

"But what if you get remarried? Carla says you'll probably get married again."

He would have laughed if it hadn't been so sad. He could imagine Angie and Carla discussing his possible marriage to another woman and speculating about what that would mean. "I'd rather you didn't listen to everything Carla tells you."

"Carla's nine going on ten, Dad. Her mom and dad split up ages ago and married other people, so she knows a lot about this."

He swallowed a chuckle. "They only divorced two years ago, honey. Regardless, if I marry someone else, your mom will always be your mom, and I will always be your dad. I'll always be here for you, Angie. I promise. You can trust in that."

She rested her head against the palm of her hand, a contented smile curving her lips. "Thanks, Dad."

"Angie, I know you were trying to matchmake a wife for me at church, but you're okay with this, aren't you? I mean, me inviting Dr. Shields over for dinner."

"Of course, Dad. It's cool. She's our doctor and she's very pretty. She doesn't mind being around a kid with a brain tumor. I like her a *lot.*"

She said it as if being their doctor made everything acceptable.

"I don't mind if you date. Carla says that's what

divorced people do." She rolled and got up off the bed. "I'd like you to date Dr. Shields."

He coughed. "Well, don't hold back, honey. Tell me how you really feel."

Even if she wanted him to date, he wasn't sure *he* was ready.

She frowned and he almost laughed at her serious expression. "Don't get too many expectations about Dr. Shields. This isn't a date—"

The telephone rang and Mark moved to the nightstand to pick up the receiver. "Hello?"

"Mark? It's Brett Anderson. How you doing, buddy?"

Mark braced his free hand against his hip and couldn't contain a smile. "Hi, Brett. I'm great. You on your way over? I invited Emma Clemmons for dinner. I thought we'd have a great visit, all of us together."

"Emmy's gonna be there?" Brett gave a bark of laughter. "Boy, I'd love to see her. I sure wish we could make it. I'm sorry, Mark, but our flight was delayed, and we're stuck in Los Angeles for the night."

"Oh, I'm sorry to hear that." Mark felt a sinking of regret. So much for a relaxed, happy group of friends.

"Can we take a rain check for another night?" Brett asked. "We should be passing through Reno again in a few months."

"Yeah, sure, Brett. Just give me a call when you'll be back in town and I'll set it up."

"Okay, and you tell Emma we said hello."

"Yeah, will do," Mark said.

"Well, I've gotta run. Take care, buddy."

"You, too, and give my best to Tina." Mark hung up the phone.

"Dad, I smell something stinky downstairs," Angie called from the bedroom door.

"What?"

"I think something's burning."

"My rolls. I forgot all about them." He dashed for the door.

With Angie close on his heels, Mark raced down the spiral stairs and into the kitchen. Sure enough, billows of smoke wafted from the oven and Mark turned it off before opening the door.

At that precise moment the doorbell rang. The dogs began to bark, scampering for the front entranceway. The smoke alarm went off, its shrill beep adding to the confusion.

"Dr. Shields is here!" Angie yelled, scurrying after the dogs.

Great timing. Emma had no idea what she was getting herself into. Burned rolls and no Brett and Tina. More than flustered, Mark reached for the pan in the oven to yank it out.

"Ow!" he yelped, dropping the pan of rolls all over the kitchen floor with a loud clatter.

"Of all the stupid things to do," he muttered as he dodged the blackened rolls littering the floor and stuck his burned fingers into his mouth to ease the pain.

How could he have been so foolish to reach into an oven without a hot pad? He needed to keep his mind on business, not his dinner guest.

No doubt hearing the commotion, Emma came into the kitchen in a flurry of blue silk. Clouds of smoke enveloped her as she flipped on the faucet and pulled him over to the sink. "Here, put your hand under the water."

Mark dipped his hand under the cold flow and felt instant relief. He breathed deep, his lungs filling with the scent of acrid smoke, his ears ringing with the noise of the smoke alarm.

So much for impressing her with a home-cooked meal.

With the pain easing, he glanced at her, finding her ravishing in a sky-blue skirt and low-heeled pumps. She'd pulled back her blond hair with a silver barrette and it curled over the tops of her shoulders with wispy bangs fringing her forehead. He had no doubt her pretty clothes would reek of smoke before she left his house tonight.

"Just stay there for a minute," Emma urged as she turned on the fan over the stove and opened the refrigerator door. "Angie, can you open those French doors to let some air in here?"

"What about flies?" Angie asked over the screech of the smoke alarm.

"We'll deal with that in a few minutes. Right now, we need some fresh air and ice."

Emma coughed and waved a hand in front of her face to clear the smoke away as Angie jerked the doors open wide. The dogs still yapped, circling Emma's legs, licking her shapely ankles.

Mark watched as Emma pushed her way past the dogs and returned to him with a handful of ice. "Where are your clean dishrags?"

Angie opened a drawer and produced a cloth and Emma wrapped it around the ice cubes before she handed it to Mark. "Hold it against your hand. It'll ease the burn."

"Thanks." Mark exhaled a breath of relief as he held the ice to his fingers.

Emma reached for the stool and climbed up to pull the cover off the smoke alarm and yank out the battery. The screaming ceased and Mark breathed with relief. Emma had handled the situation with ease.

The dogs started munching on the blackened rolls lying on the floor, making a bigger mess with the crumbs.

"Shoo! Get away," Angie yelled, and waved her arms.

"Lock them in the laundry room," Mark suggested.

With a burnt offering as enticement, Angie coerced the dogs to follow her to the back of the house.

"You must really think me incompetent." Mark gave an embarrassed chuckle as Emma knelt down and gathered up the ruined rolls, then tossed them into the garbage can.

"Not at all. I've done things like this many times myself."

"Not when you have company for dinner, I hope."

She shook her head, laughing. "Well, maybe not, but I work best under pressure. That's probably why I made such a good ER doctor."

"I can tell you're a pro in the kitchen by the way you handled my smoke alarm." He grinned and stared at the ceiling where the wires and cover dangled overhead.

"Yeah," she agreed. "I remember a Thanksgiving once when my husband's parents came into town and I almost blew up the turkey. My husband was furious—"

She froze, as if the memory was too painful to talk about. Rising to her feet, she glanced about the room. "Where's your broom?"

"I'll get it." Angie returned and hurried to the pantry. She produced a broom and Emma took it, sweeping up the last of the crumbs.

Mark stood back and watched as his daughter held the dustpan for Emma. He noticed how gentle Emma was as she steadied Angie's hands, how she explained to the girl that she should pick up the rug carefully so it wouldn't spill more crumbs back onto the floor as they took it outside to shake it off.

Never, ever, had he seen Denise speak with Angie like this or show the little girl how to tidy up. Denise usually left messes for him or the housekeeper to clean. Angie paid rapt attention to Emma, absorbing every instruction like soil soaking up rain.

Mark took a deep breath. "I'm sorry, but Brett just called to say he and Tina are stuck in Los Angeles. They won't be with us tonight."

Emma tossed him a suspicious look.

"Angie was here when I took the call," he offered lamely, hoping Emma would believe him. He felt like a teenager who had to explain himself out of a lie.

"Well, things like that happen sometimes." Emma's voice sounded vague, her expression grim. "Maybe it would be best if I leave. Your hand is burned and—"

"No!" Angie blurted. "Dad, tell her not to go."

"Please stay," he urged. "We can still have dinner, just the three of us."

Emma stared at Mark. He gave her a smile that warmed her from the inside out. She didn't think he was lying about Brett and Tina. And she couldn't very well leave him with this mess when his hand was hurting. He couldn't even wash dishes.

She tilted her head and studied him. "Okay, I'll stay."

Angie cheered and Mark exhaled a breath of relief. It had been a long time since anyone had cared enough about her to beg her to stay with them, and it lightened Emma's heart.

When she finished cleaning the floor, Emma peered at the oven and tossed a glance at Mark as she spoke in a teasing tone. "Have you got anything else in there we should salvage?"

"Yeah." He nodded with a grin. "A roast, potatoes and carrots. But I don't think I incinerated them."

She eyed his hand wrapped in the dishrag. "Well, Angie, it looks like it's you and me. Do you think you're up to the task of helping me put dinner on the table?"

Angie whooped with glee, then saluted Emma. "Yes, sir. Er, I mean, yes, ma'am."

Emma inclined her head toward the formal dining room where a table sat beneath a glittering chandelier. Mark and Angie had already set out candles and fine china on a white tablecloth. Emma's gaze swept over the dinner service for five. Suddenly she felt anxious. Without Brett and Tina here to contribute to the conversation, it might get uncomfortable. She didn't want to be a spoilsport, but doubt filled her just the same.

"Why don't you seat yourself and supervise, Mr. Williams? I think us girls can take over from here."

With a sheepish smile, Mark sat while Emma took up a hot pad and opened the oven.

"I was gonna make gravy," Mark advised. "Are the drippings burned?"

Emma lifted the golden roast from the oven and set it on top of the stove.

"Perfection," she exclaimed. "The roast and vegetables look beautiful. I count myself lucky any time a man cooks a meal for me."

A blaze of color rushed to his face, no doubt brought on by her praise. It gave her pleasure to make him feel good about his meal and she oohed and aahed as she worked, conscious of his delighted countenance.

Emma glanced at Angie. "Where's your flour, sweetie? We'll need that and some salt and pepper to mix the gravy. You don't have some garlic powder, by chance?"

"Sure, we do," Mark answered. "Angie, it's in the spice cupboard with the rest of the stuff Dr. Shields asked for."

Angie dragged the step stool over to the cupboard and opened the doors. She grunted as she lifted a container of flour and set it on the counter. Then, she reached for the salt and pepper. The child teetered on the stool and Emma braced her hand against the small of Angie's back to steady her. She stole a glance at Mark just as he came to his feet, anxiety filling his eyes.

It would have been easier for Emma to do it herself, but she wanted Angie to have the satisfaction. When children helped, it gave them a sense of accomplishment and built up their self-esteem. Emma remembered times like this with Brian and she waited patiently for Angie, somehow comforted by the little girl's presence.

The child beamed with pleasure as she handed the spices to Emma.

Ladling the potatoes and carrots into serving bowls, she then lifted the roast onto a platter. Angie pulled her stool over to the stove to stand on.

"Be careful, sweetie," Emma admonished. "I don't want you to get burned like your dad."

Angie wore an expression of awe as she listened to Emma's every word. Together, they stirred the drippings to make gravy, Emma's hand resting lightly on Angie's shoulders to keep her from falling or getting burned.

Several times, she noticed Mark came to his feet, his expression worried when Angie got too close to the burners. Each time, Emma was right there, allowing Angie to stir, yet making certain she didn't get hurt. In the deepest reaches of her soul, Emma envied Angie because the girl had such a caring and considerate father.

Mark went to the refrigerator, using his good hand to lift out a gelatin mold with fruit and whipped cream.

"I brought a green salad and a bottle of sparkling cider." Emma pointed at the counter where she had set the items earlier.

Mark hefted the bottle and gave an exaggerated lift of his brows. "What a good idea. We'll celebrate our renewed friendship."

Blowing a strand of hair out of her eyes, Emma wasn't sure what to make of this evening. She had promised herself not to get too attached to Mark and Angie and here she was, stirring gravy in their kitchen. There was no place she would rather be.

"Don't turn the heat up too high, or your gravy will burn," she instructed Angie in a gentle tone. "Keep stirring until it thickens. A medium heat works best."

"Okay." Angie whirled her whisk happily.

Her giggles filled the air and, when Emma popped a succulent piece of meat into Angie's mouth, the child chewed and swallowed without complaint. That was a good sign.

"Okay, I think we're ready to eat." Emma flipped off the stove and helped Angie down from the stool. Handing Angie a bowl of carrots, Emma carried the potatoes and meat to the table, then returned to the kitchen to retrieve the gravy.

Mark followed and they sat together. When Angie ducked her head and folded her arms, Emma was momentarily startled. She bowed her head while Mark blessed the food. As Emma unfolded her napkin and laid it in her lap, Angie copied her manners.

"Yum!" Angie exclaimed, and began to eat.

"It's good to see you hungry tonight," Mark told her.

Emma and Mark exchanged a secret smile as she passed him the butter. They were silent then, the chink of dishes and cutlery the only sounds. Emma had been counting on Brett and Tina to ease this uncomfortable silence.

"Well, I'm done." Angie tossed down her napkin and scooted back from the table. "May I be excused, please?"

For all her exclamations about being hungry, Emma noticed Angie hadn't eaten much. Mark frowned at her uneaten food and nodded his head. "Drink all your milk, then clear your dishes."

With a grimace, Angie proceeded to swallow her milk, then picked up her plate and silverware and carried them into the kitchen.

"You're very good at this," Mark observed once Angie was gone.

"What?" Emma asked.

He indicated the table. "I didn't know you were so domestic."

The heat of a blush filled her cheeks.

"I'll bet you also know how to style a little girl's hair and do the laundry without staining the whites pink," Mark observed.

Something inside her melted. "I take it you've stained your whites?"

A deep laugh rumbled in his chest. "More than just the whites. You should see what I did to Angie's yellow jumpsuit."

She was impressed that he would make the effort. "I'm sure you'll get the hang of it."

"I feel like a bumbling fool in comparison to your grace. Is there anything you can't do well?"

"Oh, yes, but you'll forgive me if I don't elaborate. From what I've seen, you're doing a great job. Your house is tidy and this roast is so tender." For some reason, she wanted to help him realize he really was doing wonderful work with Angie. Emma wished her ex-husband had been as kind and diligent as Mark.

"You're good with Angie, too. You'd make a great mother." The minute he said the words, he flushed and shut his mouth.

She froze, feeling her face drain of color. She was a mother! His words were a reminder of all she had lost. And yet, she wished she could be a mother again.

"Emma, I didn't mean I want you to—" He bit back the words.

"Of course, I understand." She hurried to her feet and reached for the dirty dishes. "Well, it's getting late."

"You don't need to do that." He stood and tried to take the plates from her.

"Don't be silly." She brushed past him. "You can't stick your injured hand in a sink full of hot water to wash these dishes. It'll take a day for the pain to subside."

He chuckled. "I usually cheat and pop them into the dishwasher."

"Some of them will have to be scrubbed. If Angie comes back, I'll let her help."

"That's what I meant, Emma." He followed her into the kitchen, carrying the salad bowl with his uninjured hand. "You're so good with Angie. She seems to listen to you more than she does me. I wish I had your magic touch."

She hesitated. "I'm sure she misses her mother, so she pays more attention when a woman's around. But there's no doubt she loves you, Mark."

She turned on the faucet and rinsed the dishes. He stood beside her, taking the plates and glasses one by one and placing them in the dishwasher. With his shoulder brushing against hers, a companionable silence settled over them. She felt as though she had come home after being gone a very long time.

"Thanks for being here tonight, Emma. Even before the divorce, Denise was too busy with her new boyfriend."

"Boyfriend?"

"Yeah. You know Denise." He put the salt and pepper shakers in the cupboard.

Yes, she knew Denise.

He released a deep sigh. "She never wanted a baby. When she found out she was pregnant with Angie, she wanted to get rid of it, but I talked her out of it. When Angie lost her hair, she claimed she was too embarrassed to be seen out in public with her own daughter."

That explained Angie's self-consciousness over her bald head.

"I'm so sorry, Mark."

He shrugged. "Yeah, me, too. It wouldn't be so bad if Denise came to visit Angie once in a while."

"She doesn't visit her daughter?"

He shook his head.

Emma's eyes widened. "Not at all?"

Again, he shook his head. "I've tried to reach her numerous times, but I don't have a phone number for her anymore. I usually end up leaving a message with her mother." He shrugged. "Who knows if she delivers the messages to Denise or not?"

Anger caused Emma to stiffen her shoulders. "I can't comprehend how Denise could turn her back on her own child. How could she abandon such a sweet, beautiful girl like Angie? I'd give anything in the world if I could—"

Tears filled her eyes and she ducked her head, the water from the faucet rushing over her trembling hands. She didn't move for several moments, trying to regain her composure. She bit the inside of her mouth, crushing the words she had been ready to blurt.

Inhaling a deep breath, he let it out slowly. "I didn't mean to upset you, Emma."

She shook her head. "I'm fine."

He gave her a soothing smile. "It's been good for Angie to have a woman in the house, treating her with patience and kindness. That's what being a woman is all about."

Emma didn't look up. His praise both humbled and surprised her. Her ex-husband had never said such things to her. Instead he'd found plenty to criticize. Nothing she did ever seemed right.

"What about you, Emma?" Mark waited while she lifted her head and her gaze locked with his. "Tell me about you and David."

Hurt flashed through her like a silver bullet to her heart. "We were married eight years. Now we're divorced. End of story."

He opened his mouth to pursue the subject, but she flipped on the garbage disposal, cutting off any further questions.

Chapter Ten

The following Tuesday, Emma couldn't deny the dread that settled in her stomach. Mark and Angie were coming in for a treatment and she caught herself looking at her watch repeatedly.

She had been so rude to Mark last week when he'd asked about her divorce. Up to that point, she had thoroughly enjoyed having dinner in his beautiful home, helping out when he injured his hand, teaching Angie to make gravy.

Discussing her divorce had not been on the agenda. It would have lead to other topics she wasn't prepared to address. Instead, she'd finished cleaning the kitchen, mumbled an excuse about getting up early in the morning, and beat a hasty retreat.

She tried to tell herself she didn't care if she saw Mark and Angie today. Sonja would give Angie her treatment. Emma would pop in afterward to ask how the Marinol was working, then get on with her job. She didn't want to see them.

Who was she kidding? She could hardly wait to see them. That was the problem.

"Oh, just shoot me." She leaned her head against the palm of her hand.

"Did you say something, Dr. Shields?" Darcy asked from behind the front reception counter.

"No, I wasn't speaking to you," Emma snapped.

Darcy flinched and ducked her head over her keyboard.

Emma walked down the hall, determined to forget Mark would be here any minute. She shouldn't be so sharp with Darcy. Maybe she should apologize.

She kept walking.

By ten-thirty, Sonja came to advise her that Angie was finished with her treatment and that she and Mark waited in the examination room.

Emma inhaled a deep, steadying breath. Angie was just a patient and her father an old school friend. Nothing more.

"Hello," Emma greeted them as she entered the room and closed the door.

Mark sat on the bed, holding Angie on his lap. Dressed in black slacks, he also wore a white shirt and yellow tie. He must have come from work. Clean-shaven, he had combed his hair back. He looked good.

Angie curled against his chest, her flowered hat lying next to Mark's thigh on the bed. She sniffed and wiped her nose, her eyes red and puffy.

Emma's heart tore into a thousand pieces.

"What's the matter, sweetie?" Emma asked. "Didn't the Emla Cream work today?"

Mark gave Emma a reassuring smile. "It worked fine.

She's upset because the rest of her hair is falling out. It had just started to grow back."

Angie hiccupped and rubbed her eyes before she pointed at her right temple. "See? My braid fell out. The kids in my neighborhood run away when I go outside. They say I'm a sick-o and they don't want to play with me. Carla's gone back to Nebraska, so now I have no friends at all."

Sympathy filled Emma. It must be so difficult for Angie to live with this illness.

"Would it do any good to have me come and talk to them and explain that your illness isn't contagious?" Emma asked.

Why had she offered that? *Dumb, dumb, dumb!*

Mark shifted his weight and gave a sad smile. "That's very generous, Emma, but I don't think it's necessary. I can explain it to them."

"Will my hair grow back, Emma?" Angie asked with a sniffle.

Emma.

"Angie, you shouldn't call an adult by their first name," Mark said.

"It's okay, Mark. I give Angie my permission to call me Emma, if it's all right with you." Somehow, she didn't mind.

Mark nodded and Angie mustered up a small smile.

"Now, back to your question. Of course your hair will grow back, honey. You're beautiful, even without your hair. Some top models shave their heads on purpose. Many people consider it quite lovely." Emma read between the lines. Angie longed for her mother's approval. Without her hair, she believed her mother wouldn't love her.

Angie's eyes widened. "Really?"

"Absolutely. Remember what I told you about the drugs killing good things as well as bad?"

Angie nodded, her eyes still filled with tears.

"Well, one of those good things is hair. As soon as we finish your chemo, your hair will grow right back, maybe even thicker than before, and I doubt you'll be able to see any of the scars. Until then, are you interested in wearing a wig?"

"A wig?" Angie crinkled her nose with repugnance.

"Yeah, I can get you a referral for a nice wig that will look quite natural."

Angie shook her head, her upper lip curled.

"Okay, then you can just pretend you're a sumo wrestler. Of course, we'll have to fatten you up some more."

Angie wiped her nose with the back of her hand. "A sumo wrestler?"

Emma envisioned this frail child stomping around in a muscleman crouch with a fierce look on her face, wearing what looked like a baggy diaper. "Sure! Why not?"

Angie hopped off Mark's lap and posed in the exact posture Emma had just imagined, minus the diaper. The sight of the skinny little girl stooped and flexing her scrawny muscles and puffing out her cheeks was hilarious. Emma threw back her head and laughed.

Mark chuckled and shook his head. "Now, that's a scary scene."

Angie giggled and came over to hold out her pinky finger to Emma. "Pinky promise my hair will grow back?"

Locking her pinky with Angie's, Emma gave a gentle jerk. "Pinky promise."

Angie threw her arms around Emma's neck and hugged tight. Unprepared for the contact, Emma flinched. Then, she squeezed the child back. A rush of emotion washed over Emma.

"Oh, thank you, Emma," Angie said. "I love you."

Emma almost dropped her clipboard. Like a pointed dart, Angie's arms and words sent a shot of heat straight to Emma's heart. She caught the warm, sweet smell of Angie's skin and had to close her eyes as wave after wave of sentiment pounded against her.

Warning chimes sounded in Emma's head.

She pulled Angie's arms away and smiled at the girl. "Now, you go out and see what surprise Sonja has in her special stash while I talk to your father, okay?"

"Okay!" Angie opened the door and went out into the hallway.

"Thanks for that," Mark said, his eyes shining. "I can't tell you how much she yearns for a woman's approval."

"Maybe Denise will visit her soon."

Emotion covered his face and his voice caught as he looked away. This was the strong, in-control Mark Williams from high school? Somehow, Emma felt very close to him, and she didn't like it.

The room was suddenly very hot. She needed out—now!

Emma stood and moved toward the door. It was best to end this conversation. Her other patients never confided so much to her. Yet, Mark and Angie were somehow special and she found herself thinking about them at all times of the day. When they were gone, she missed them, for crying out loud!

"I'll see you Thursday night at the Make-A-Wish meeting," she said as she stepped away.

"Yeah, I'll be there."

She hurried down the hall to another examination room where her next patient waited. Sounds of people talking in the treatment room filtered over the low hum of machinery.

Mark walked past, heading toward the front receptionist desk. Emma knew he would schedule Angie's next appointment before he left.

Taking the file from the holder affixed to the door, Emma read it to bring herself up to date on the next patient's case. As she stood there, Christy's voice reached her from the front counter.

"Did you ask for Friday off?"

Emma glanced up and saw Christy and Tom, two of her nurses, standing by the reception desk, their backs toward her. Mark stopped beside the counter and waited for Darcy to get off the phone so she could schedule Angie's next appointment. Angie stood close by, twirling a green top she had gotten from Sonja's stash of toys.

"Nah, I don't dare ask The Ogre for any time off," Tom responded to Christy's question. "The last time I did, she almost took my head off."

"Ogre?" Christy gave a sarcastic laugh. "Can a woman be an ogre?"

Tom chuckled. "Okay, *ogress.* At least, I think she's female. When's the last time *you* asked Dr. Shields for time off work?"

"Hmm." Christy lifted a hand to rest on her hip. "I don't remember, but I've sure worked a lot of overtime."

"Yeah, we all have," Tom agreed. "I'd quit if she didn't pay us so well."

Emma saw Mark shift his weight, a frown pulling at his brows. He had heard every word. So had Angie. The little girl's mouth pursed in disapproval as she peered at Christy over the top of the counter.

Angry heat crept up Emma's neck and face.

Spying Emma, Angie came down the hall toward her. Panic replaced the anger as Emma stared at the child.

Sonja came from the supply room and flashed a stern look at Tom and Christy. "Get back to work, please."

The two turned and saw Emma standing there, and ducked their heads as they scurried away. The cowards.

"Emma?" Angie came to stand just in front of her.

"Yes?" Her tight voice was an indicator of her strangled throat.

"Why did they call you an ogre?"

Fury and embarrassment burned inside Emma's stomach when she thought of her staff calling her names in front of the patients.

A tinge of doubt shadowed her mind. Maybe it was true. It was a revelation to find out exactly what her employees thought of her. Obviously, they didn't like her much.

How could she blame them when she didn't like herself?

Anger mingled with hurt when she considered what she should do about it. She opened her mouth, but no words came from her parched throat.

"Come on, Angie. It's time to go," Mark called as he held out his hand.

Angie's brow furrowed with persistence as she stared at Emma. "Well, *I* don't think you're an ogre. I love you."

Angie went to her father and Emma stared after her. She wanted to weep, but crying was for weak people, and she couldn't be weak—couldn't show that she was anything but strong. She wouldn't have survived losing Brian and David and still be able to run her busy medical office if she hadn't been strong.

Her gaze locked with Mark's. His eyes crinkled with—

Pity!

She hardened her eyes. He could keep his sympathy. She wanted to yell at him to go home and leave her alone. She didn't need his compassion or his sweet little daughter who insisted she loved her. She didn't need *anyone!*

Who was she kidding? All the sleepless nights, prowling the confines of her small apartment, wishing she had someone to talk to, someone to confide in.

But she hated being hurt even more.

Clenching her jaw, she went back to work. Later that evening, when all the patients and staff were gone and the whirr of machines silenced, Emma sat alone in her office. As was her routine, Sonja came in to say good-night before she left for the day.

"Do you need anything else, Dr. Shields?" Sonja asked with a smile.

"Just one thing." Removing her glasses, Emma took a shaky breath and let it out slowly. "Tomorrow, I want you to direct the office staff to use more discretion before calling me names in front of the patients."

Sonja's face reddened. "I'm sorry, Doctor. I've already had that discussion with them. Don't pay any attention to it."

"Yes, well, I doubt it inspires much confidence in our patients. If Christy and Tom can't keep their feelings to themselves, they can leave. No one's forcing them to work here. And I would appreciate it if you stop scheming with Larry Meacham to get me involved in things like Make-A-Wish. I don't appreciate your meddling and I don't need more things to do."

Sonja gaped at Emma, hurt filling her eyes as she chewed her lower lip.

Emma stared right back, silently daring Sonja to deny the accusations and—

Sonja looked away, a sad light glimmering in her eyes. Was she crying?

"Yes, you're right, Doctor. I have no right to interfere in your life. And I'll speak with Tom and Christy again, to make certain they understand what you expect."

"Thank you." Emma pushed the spectacles up on her nose and picked up a file, pretending to thumb through the paperwork.

The words blurred before her eyes.

Sonja pivoted to go but hesitated. Emma threw her a quick look. Yes, there definitely were tears glistening in Sonja's eyes.

Sonja spoke in a tentative voice that grew stronger. "Emma, I never told you that I promised Brian I'd look after you. He made me promise I'd do everything I could to help you get over his death. That little boy wanted you happy. It made it easier for him, knowing I'd do what I could to help you go on living."

A rush of tears filled Emma's eyes and a hollow sob escaped her throat.

"Late at night, when he couldn't sleep because of the

pain, Brian spent hours talking about you. I think that's the reason he lasted so long—he knew how much it would hurt his mommy when he died."

Emma couldn't respond. Her throat felt strangled with tears.

Sonja took a deep, trembling breath. "I care a great deal for you, Emma. You should get out more, meet nice men like Mr. Williams, get married again, and raise a family. You used to be different when Brian was alive. You were happy. Brian's the one who died, not you. And if it gets me fired for saying so, someone needs to tell you."

Turning, Sonja didn't wait for Emma to say anything before she left the room.

Emma stared at the closed door for several moments, then tossed her pen and glasses aside as she sat back in her chair. She couldn't breathe, couldn't even think.

"Well, I guess I deserved that," Emma muttered to herself.

She stared at the mountain of files stacked in neat rows on her desk, not really seeing it.

Forget it. She was sick of work and weary of this office. She was tired of sorrow.

She dug her purse out of the bottom drawer of her desk, then stood up. She flipped off the light, locked the door, then hurried out to her car. As she fumbled with the keys, her hands shook. Finally she unlocked the door, got in, then drove out of the parking lot.

A hoarse moan rose in her chest as she entered the freeway. Tears poured down her cheeks. A scream of pain tore from her throat. Not physical pain, but an excruciating torture of the soul. As if she were being pulled apart from the inside.

Again and again, she screamed until sobs racked her body and she had to pull over so she wouldn't cause an accident.

Ogre!

Yes, that's what she felt like inside. A horrid, ugly monster.

If Mark Williams could face a nasty divorce and the possibility of losing his daughter, why couldn't she face tomorrow with a bit of dignity, warmth and compassion?

Oh, God, please help me! If You're really there as Mark says You are, help me find my way. I'm so lonely. I'm so lost.

It was the first time she had prayed since the night Brian died. Sitting alone in her car, on the busy freeway as cars zipped past, she felt suddenly—

At peace.

A calm sensation enveloped her like a warm blanket. Maybe she imagined it. It couldn't be real.

Her heart lightened and tears of joy poured down her cheeks. Somehow, she didn't feel quite so lost or abandoned anymore. Deep inside, she knew Mark was right. She'd hidden herself from the Lord out of anger and hurt, but it didn't change the truth.

God lived. He was there, loving and caring for her. Waiting for her to return to Him.

"What have I become?" she cried with remorse, leaning her forehead against the steering wheel.

Feeling wretched didn't give her the right to make others miserable, too. When she remembered all the sharp words and curt reprimands she had thrown at her office staff over the past years, she wanted to hide in shame. Before Brian's death, she had always been so kind and patient with others. Like that night at Mark's house when she had taught Angie to make gravy. But now, she was an ogre.

Something must change.

Whatever happened next, she wanted to be kinder, more generous. That didn't mean she would start dating, but maybe it was time to give Tom and Christy a day off. They'd earned it, even though they were smart-mouthed kids. And maybe she'd ask Darcy to start planning a summer barbecue for the office staff and their families. Maybe this year, they'd have a Christmas party. They'd never had one before. And why not?

Because laughter might crack The Ogre's face.

They said laughter healed wounded hearts. Emma had laughed more the past few weeks since Mark and Angie had come into her life than she had in the past two years since Brian's death.

She dabbed at her eyes with a tissue, feeling like a reformed Scrooge. A slightly hysterical giggle bubbled up inside her. What a fool she had been, hoarding the kindness in her heart like a shroud of death.

No, not Scrooge. Just an embittered woman who had lost her way. She didn't like the person she had become.

Time for a change. Setting limits was okay. She could be nice without becoming close to others.

Or could she?

She wiped her eyes, blew her nose, then pulled her car back onto the freeway and drove home.

Somehow, Emma's resolve made her stronger. With Sonja and Mark's examples, she could stand to live again. To feel. To hope.

How ironic that the boy who had broken her heart in high school was mending it back together piece by piece.

She could repay him by trying to heal his precious daughter.

Emma clutched the steering wheel tight and mouthed another prayer.

Please, God, don't let me fail this time.

Chapter Eleven

"Here's those reports you asked for, Doctor."

Emma looked up and found Tom standing over her, holding a stack of manila folders jam-packed with papers.

Emma took the reports and set them on her desk. "Thank you."

He turned to go.

"Um, Tom? I understand you've been hoping to take a week off this summer to go camping with your family."

He paused beside the door, his ears reddening. "Yeah, but, I don't really need to if—"

"I think it's a wonderful idea, Tom. You've worked hard and deserve a break. Why don't you take two weeks? Just submit your request in writing to Sonja."

Emma looked down at the manila folders and opened one of the reports, pretending to read it.

"Uh, thanks, Dr. Shields. Wow! I really appreciate it."

Surprise and appreciation filled Tom's voice. He left her office, pulling the door closed. Emma heard his unmistakable whoop of delight as he made a hasty retreat.

Joy speared Emma's heart. She had almost forgotten the contentment it brought when she made other people happy. Perhaps there were additional changes she could make.

She reached for a notebook and pen, determined to start right away.

Mark led Angie into the main hallway of Emma's office. It was seven-thirty in the morning and Angie was the first patient of the day.

Looking up, Mark saw Tom standing just inside the break room holding a coffee mug in one hand, a newspaper in the other. The door was slightly ajar. Though Mark couldn't see her, he could hear Darcy's voice as she spoke to Tom.

"I don't know what's gotten into her. She's sure different."

The air smelled of the customary scent of antiseptic mingled with freshly brewed coffee. Though Emma didn't drink coffee, she kept it on hand for her patients and employees.

"Yeah, she even gave me two weeks off to go camping with my family."

"Well, she's got me planning a barbecue for the office staff, their families and some of our patients at Fernandez Park in two weeks. And Sonja mentioned year-end bonuses for all the employees."

Tom's brows quirked at this news. "Bonuses? Wow!"

Quietly listening to this conversation, Mark shifted his weight and set Angie's MRIs on the counter as he signed in on the clipboard kept by the front desk. Angie sidled closer to his leg, slipping her hand into his. She'd pulled her flowered hat low around her ears, self-conscious of her bald head.

Tom slapped the newspaper against his thigh. "I've worked here almost two years and we've never had an office party. Have you ever seen Dr. Shields like this?"

They were talking about Emma again. For some reason, it made Mark angry and defensive. He didn't like them talking behind Emma's back, and yet this was good news he heard.

"Nope." Darcy looked pointedly toward Emma's office door, which was closed. "What do you think made the difference?"

Tom laughed and wiped his hands down the front of his blue smock. "Maybe she's got a new boyfriend. I hope he sticks around for a long time."

A boyfriend? He didn't think so. Emma would have mentioned it to him.

Wouldn't she?

Somehow their souls connected in a way he couldn't explain. He missed her and wished she could spend more time with him and Angie.

If he got close to her, would she hurt him? He couldn't stand another failed relationship. Losing her mother had been hard on Angie and he wouldn't bring another woman into her life to abandon her again at the first sign of trouble.

"I hope she does have a boyfriend. It'll take her mind off us," Darcy said.

Tom grinned. "Well, I guess now we'll have to call her something besides The Ogre."

Mark opened his mouth, prepared to let them know what he thought of their name-calling. Emma deserved better than this and he—

"How about calling her the Boss? Remember, she signs your checks." Sonja caught them off guard when she came from the supply room carrying boxes of syringes and cotton balls. She stood in the doorway of the break room and flashed them a stern look, her voice filled with warning.

"Sorry, Sonja," Darcy said. "We didn't mean any harm. We really appreciate the changes Dr. Shields has made. She's just so different lately."

"I'm glad you've noticed, now get back to work," Sonja said.

Darcy walked out of the break room and returned to her desk where she started tapping away on her keyboard. A satisfied smile curved Tom's lips as he also exited the break room and whistled his way down the hall.

Seeing Angie, Sonja bent at the waist so she could greet the child at eye level. "Hi, sweetheart. How are you doing?"

Angie nodded but kept her cheek pressed against Mark's thigh, no sparkle in her hollow eyes. "Fine."

"Good. Have you got your EMLA patch on?"

Angie nodded and pressed her hand to her chest. "Yep, Daddy put it on for me."

"Okay, let's wait for Mrs. Valdez to get here and then I'll take you down the hall."

Mr. and Mrs. Valdez entered the reception room a few minutes later and Angie's eyes brightened as she hurried over to take Mrs. Valdez's hand. As usual, no words were needed between these two kindred spirits.

Mrs. Valdez had lost substantial weight, her intense chemo protocol taking its toll on her body. Angie didn't seem to notice.

"Okay, let's get started." Sonja led them all into the treatment room.

As was his routine, Mark translated for Sonja and she got Mrs. Valdez set up with an IV drip.

Angie stayed close by, holding Mrs. Valdez's free hand, patting the woman's shoulder now and then.

"Okay, Angie, let me go get your injection, and I'll be right back," Sonja said as she left the room.

When Emma poked her head around the door, Mark looked up. Dressed in a light pink skirt and white blouse with purple and yellow pansies embroidered along the collar, she wore her hair long and curling against the top of her shoulders. What a change. Where was the stern hairstyle and clothing? Without the severe clip at the back of her neck, she looked stunning. He was half tempted to invite her to the movies Friday night.

He noticed tenderness filled Emma's eyes as she stared at Angie and Mrs. Valdez. "So, how are my two favorite patients?"

Her gaze swerved over to Mark and suddenly a veil dropped over her eyes. The cold, professional doctor had returned. And yet, when they'd gone shopping together and she'd come to his house for dinner, he'd felt a strong connection with her. Had he only imagined it?

"Okay, Angie, we're ready for you," she called.

"Ah, do I have'ta?" Angie groaned.

"Yes, I'm sorry, champ," Mark said.

Careful not to bump the IV in Mrs. Valdez's arm, Angie slid off the woman's lap and walked over to Emma. Mark picked up the packet of MRIs and followed as the doctor led them down the hall.

Inside the examination room, Angie lay back against the pillow on the couch and stared at the wall. Sonja came in and administered the injection. When Sonja asked Angie to pick a toy out of her special stash, Angie refused.

"No, thank you." Her voice sounded small.

Sonja's brows lifted in surprise. "You don't want anything today? But I've got some new coloring books."

Angie shook her head and looked away.

"Why so gloomy?" Emma asked.

Mark handed the large packet of MRI scans to Emma. She held them dumbly, wondering what he wanted her to do with them.

"Angie's been on the chemo for two months and there's no shrinkage of the tumor." His gaze didn't meet Emma's. "The neurosurgeon was disappointed."

So was Mark, if Emma read the concern in his eyes correctly. She hoped he didn't blame her for the lack of shrinkage. She had explicitly followed the protocol given to her by the doctors at U.C.S.F., yet she felt responsible. Her ex-husband's accusations jangled inside her mind and she dreaded hearing the same from Mark.

Emma pulled out the scans, holding them up to the overhead lighting. She never looked at MRI scans for her other patients. That was the neurosurgeon's job. This time, she had to see for herself.

"Scan after scan shows no change." Mark stood close beside her, pointing at the hazy-white tumor, which was big as a plump grape. The tumor was not very large when compared to fruit, but when it was inside a child's head, it was enormous and deadly.

"Has the neurosurgeon said there's been more growth?" Emma asked.

His nearness caused her heart to hammer against her chest.

Mark shook his head as he stared at Angie's hands folded in her lap. The child stared at the wall. "No, thank goodness. No growth, no shrinkage. We're at a standstill."

He stepped back and Emma breathed with relief, hardly able to think with him standing so close.

"Well, that's a good sign. We've stopped the growth. Now, we just need time to back it up and shrink the tumor."

She spoke in a confident tone, but her hands trembled and she found it difficult to respond in a professional manner. She refused to believe Angie would die. God wouldn't fail her again.

Or would He?

"Don't be discouraged, you two," she admonished lightly. "We've only just begun treatment and it's quite common this early in the process for there to be no shrinkage. It takes time for the drugs to get through the blood-brain barrier."

"Blood-brain barrier?" Mark asked.

"Yes, it's the body's natural defense to keep impurities out of the brain. I think this is a positive sign. We've stopped the tumor from growing and now it will start to shrink."

A flicker of hope flashed in Mark's eyes and he blew out a deep huff of air. "I can't tell you how relieved I am to hear that."

She already knew. When Brian had been ill, she'd clung to every thread of hope the doctors offered. But how could she encourage this man and his daughter when she herself feared Angie might die? Those were the odds.

Trust in Me, and I will show you the way.

The words filled her heart, giving her more confidence. Her fledgling faith in God burgeoned like a tiny seed planted in fertile soil. The opposite of faith was worry and she decided to trust in the Lord.

Just once more.

"How often is your neurosurgeon requesting MRI's?" she asked.

"Twice a month," Mark replied. "It if starts to shrink, he said we'd go to once a month. Do you really think we just need more time for the tumor to shrink?"

"Absolutely!" Emma's voice was filled with as much enthusiasm as she could muster.

Never in her career had she *ever* responded in such a manner. She didn't want to get sued if the chemo didn't work. It was almost as if an outside force directed her to speak the words.

I am the resurrection and the life. He that believeth in Me, though he were dead, yet shall he live.

She needed to prepare Mark for what could happen when the protocol ended, but she didn't want to speak so bluntly in front of the child.

"Angie, why don't you go with Sonja while I talk to your dad?"

"Ooo-kay." Pressing her lips together, Angie slid off the couch and shuffled out the door.

Emma stared at her clipboard, wondering how to begin.

"Mark, I think you need to know the most we can expect is a twenty percent shrinkage. And you can expect the tumor to begin growing again within two years after the protocol is completed. Of course, there are exceptions. I'm just telling you the odds."

Mark's face whitened, his words filled with trepidation. "And if it starts to grow again?"

"We'll determine how we should proceed when we come to that point. Every child is different. We just don't know for certain how Angie's body will react to the treatments. I'm just telling you what happens with the majority of children with this type of tumor."

"Will Angie need to have MRI's the rest of her life?" he asked.

"Yes, I'm sorry. The good thing is, if there's no growth after we shrink the tumor, your neurosurgeon will probably request fewer MRIs. No matter what, Angie will always need an annual MRI, just to keep an eye on what's happening inside her pretty head." Emma tried to smile, hoping to alleviate the distress her words caused.

Her heart went out to Mark. Angie had an illness that would need to be carefully monitored the rest of her life. The sleeping giant in her head could awaken at any time. After the chemotherapy, there could be hormone and kidney damage.

Emma tried to show a reassuring smile. "Really, you mustn't be discouraged. Give the protocol time to work. It's going to be okay."

She'd done it again, saying things she shouldn't. Giving him false hope when she didn't know for certain what might happen.

Mark faced Emma and she couldn't mistake the tone of panic in his voice. "Emma, what if the tumor doesn't respond to the chemo? What if it starts to grow again?"

She dreaded this question. If Angie died, he'd blame her, just like David did after Brian died.

Taking a deep breath, Emma chose her words carefully. "Miracles have been known to happen, and you and Angie are due for a big one."

"Yes, but I'm also a realist. God could take her from me, and I don't know if I can handle that. I can't lose her—" He pinched the bridge of his nose and squeezed his eyes shut. "I feel so helpless, Emma."

She inhaled a shaky breath and let it go. "Remember what you told me that day we went shopping at the warehouse?"

"I remember." His voice sounded hoarse with emotion.

"Well, if you're right and God is real, how can you doubt Him? He's the only one that can save her, Mark. Not me. Not the drugs. Just Him."

An invisible energy folded around her, filling her with the courage to believe what she said. She didn't know why God had taken her precious son from her, or why he allowed tragedies to happen to innocent people, but she realized He wanted her to learn to trust in Him. From His perspective, Brian wasn't dead. The little boy had returned home.

Mark's brow crinkled with thought. "How did you cope with your divorce?"

The words fell against her heart like a ten ton sledge.

"I didn't. David blamed me for—" Her voice broke and she tried again. "David blamed me for so many things, and I blamed myself, too. Looking back at my marriage, I wonder now if David ever loved me at all, or just wanted to marry me because I could get him in doors he couldn't open on his own. You might say I was his trophy wife."

That was the main reason she didn't want to become involved with Mark. He'd married Denise Johnson for the same reason: because she looked good on his arm. Emma wanted more. She wanted someone to love her for herself, not for prestige or wealth.

"I came to realize I deserved better than to be married to a man who disliked me," she said.

Mark's quizzical expression showed his confusion. "You're right about that, Emma. And yet, you still wear his ring. I thought you still loved the guy."

"It's my 'no pest' strip." She gave a shaky laugh. "It keeps men from hitting on me."

She had confided much more than she'd intended. A small part of her wished she and Mark could be close again—

"So…Darcy can get you set up with your next appointment," she hedged.

His eyes filled with unasked questions, but she didn't want to answer them. She headed for the door.

"How can you lecture me about God, Emma? You live in your sterile world with no one to care about and nothing to lose. It sounds very comfortable and safe."

A lash of pain ripped through her chest and she anchored her grip on the doorknob. It hurt so bad, she thought there must be blood on the floor. If only he knew all she had lost, he'd eat his words.

She turned to leave.

"Emma, I'm sorry. I shouldn't have said that. It's just that I'm afraid."

She hesitated, her back to him. It must have taken a lot for him to admit his fear and to apologize for hurting her. Neither the old Mark nor David would have done such a thing.

"No, you're right, Mark. I've tried to keep myself

safe so I won't be hurt again." She glanced at him from over her shoulder. Her heart melted at the site of his handsome face torn with anguish. "But my plan failed the moment you and Angie walked into my life."

Stepping out into the hall, she headed straight for her office, praying he didn't try to stop her. She didn't know what she'd do if he pushed the issue.

Her heart pounded. Three more steps and she entered her sanctuary, closing the door behind her. Leaning her head against the smooth paneling, she tried to steady her rapid breathing.

She laughed out loud. What good was she to Mark when she couldn't be strong for herself? And yet, something had broken loose inside her. Something she didn't understand. She was consumed with the desire to help heal Angie and to believe the Lord wanted the best for them. Something else sat on the fringes of her mind. Something she couldn't understand.

Please, God! Please help me save this child.

Would God answer her simple prayer this time?

I am here, my child. I have heard every plea from your heart.

Emma gasped and looked around. The words sounded as clear as if someone stood right beside her, speaking into her ear.

"Show me the way, Heavenly Father. Please show me what I must do to help Angie."

A flash of insight opened in her mind. It speared her with such powerful intelligence and light that her entire being filled with it. Within seconds, she knew what she should do, what treatment she should suggest to the doctors at U.C.S.F.

Of course! She should have thought of it before. It seemed so simple and yet it had eluded her and the other doctors.

The next step would be the hardest she had ever taken. She had resolved to trust in God, but what if she failed again? What if she was wrong?

You will not fail. I am with you.

No longer hesitant, she walked to her desk, then picked up the telephone and dialed the number for Larry Meacham at the U.C.S.F. hospital. If this was what the Lord wanted, then she must have faith. Angie's life depended on it.

Chapter Twelve

Friday was a hectic day. Instead of going golfing or attending conferences like other doctors, Emma kept her office open for appointments. Work kept her from dwelling on Mark and Angie.

By three o'clock in the afternoon, she found herself longing to seek some sunshine and fresh air. Her last patient had just left, so she stunned herself and her staff by giving them the rest of the day off. Their gasps of pleasure delighted her and she smiled as they shut off their computers and dashed for their purses and car keys.

After she locked up the office, Emma headed out on McCarran Boulevard, driving toward Highland Cemetery.

Thump, thump, thump!

Now what?

She pulled off to the side of the road and got out to inspect her car.

A flat tire.

She took a deep inhale of hot summer air. Cars

whizzed past, but not a service station or convenience store in site. Being stranded on the road in this heat was not her idea of fun.

She wiped beads of perspiration from her upper lip and considered her options. Could she fix the tire herself?

No, she had no idea where to begin.

Call her ex-husband?

He'd resent her for pulling him away from work. She'd rather try to change it herself.

What about roadside service? She had coverage through her insurance company, but it always took so long. In this heat, the wait could prove miserable.

She popped the engine hood to signal she was in trouble, then got back in the car and reached for her cell phone. When she called the service, they confirmed her fear it would take a while for a mechanic to arrive.

So much for her free afternoon.

She settled in for the long haul, running the air conditioner, her hands resting on the steering wheel. She stared out her windshield, wishing she had a book to read.

Sunshine blazed across the brown hills surrounding the city and she longed for the water bottle she'd left sitting on her desk. Closing her eyes, she let her mind wander. Bitter memories swamped her as she recalled years earlier when she and Brian had been stranded with a flat. When her husband arrived, he'd berated her for driving over a nail, as if she'd done it on purpose.

The sound of a car close by caused her to open her eyes. A blue Lexus pulled up behind her and she tensed, sitting up straight. She pressed the lock button on the door and reached for her phone. Though the road was quite busy, she wanted to play it safe.

A tall, slender man got out of the Lexus. Her pulse sped up and a warm sensation flowed over her as she tilted her head to get a better look in her rearview mirror. He sauntered toward her car in that confident, self-assured amble she'd committed to memory years earlier.

"Oh, no." She groaned and leaned her forehead against the steering wheel.

Mark Williams wearing a dark suit and tie tapped on the glass and she lifted her head. As her eyes locked with his, he flashed her a dimpled smile and she rolled the window down.

"Hi, there." He sounded so friendly she couldn't help smiling back. "I was just passing by on the other side and thought it looked like you over here. You broken down?"

Relief, fear, happiness and dread fogged her brain. She tried to make sense of it all and decided to feel relieved for the time being.

"Yeah, I've got a flat."

"You got a spare?" He took off his jacket and slung it over his shoulder, looking more handsome than a man had a right to.

"I think so, but I just called a roadside service."

"Call them back and cancel. By the time they get here, I'll have it changed. Pop the trunk, will you?"

Without waiting for her reply, he walked to his car where he tossed his jacket through the open window onto the front seat, pulled his tie free and rolled up the sleeves of his white shirt. She popped the trunk and reached for her phone, then got out of her car. As she dialed the number for the roadside service, she stood there watching Mark work.

Like a pro mechanic, he rummaged around in her trunk for the jack and spare tire.

"Well, this is a big change." She couldn't keep the amusement from her voice as she pocketed her phone and came to stand beside him.

He grunted as he lifted the new tire from her trunk. "What is?"

"You changing a flat tire. I seem to remember you got hauled into the principal's office for letting the air out of Mr. Needham's tires on more than one occasion."

Mr. Needham had been their geometry teacher and all the kids in school had hated him.

Mark gave a deep laugh. He had a streak of grease on his chin. "Yeah, I remember that. I had to dump the trash and clean every chalkboard in the school for two months. The only reason I didn't get suspended was because we had a regional playoff the next day and they needed me on the team."

How true. With Mark's natural athletic ability, he had led their football team to a state championship every year. No way was the school principal about to jeopardize that victory because of Mr. Needham's flat tires.

"I think you let the air out of Gary Crane's tires, too."

Gary had been the school nerd, and Mark had picked on him for no other reason.

He met her eyes and she saw remorse in their green depths. "Yeah, I'm sorry about that. I wasn't too nice back then and I really regret it. I could have made Gary's life easier, not more difficult. I wish I could make it up to him somehow."

His admission stunned her. As he turned his attention back to her car, she didn't argue, but he seemed so different now. So friendly, generous and real. The man of her dreams. Yet, she had learned long ago that dreams rarely came true.

While Mark worked, she couldn't help admiring his muscled arms. "I hate to put you out and get your hands and clothes dirty."

"No worry, they'll clean up fine." His voice sounded muffled as he bent over the jack and began to loosen the bolts. "There's your problem."

"What?"

He pointed and she stood beside him. "Your tires are bald. You can see the steel belts coming through."

She peered at the shimmer of steel on the flat tire and wondered why she hadn't noticed before. A quick glance at her other tires told her they weren't in much better shape.

With a flip of his long fingers, Mark spun a bolt free. "As soon as you get the chance, you should take your car into a dealer and change all your other tires. You don't want to face winter roads on these wheels."

She agreed. "Yes, thank you for pointing it out. If you hadn't said something, I would have continued driving on them."

"You're welcome. Most husbands take care of these things."

She snorted.

"I take it your husband was the exception. He didn't like to be bothered?"

Yes, that described David perfectly.

"Are you kidding? I've always taken my own car in for service and filled my own tank with gasoline. I guess I've neglected it lately."

Mark worked for a time in silence and she watched with rapt attention. Thinking it might help if she found herself in this predicament again, she began asking lots of questions about the process. He answered patiently and she felt drawn to the deep timbre of his voice.

Once he got the flat tire off, he rolled it away and wiped his damp brow with his forearm. He lifted the new tire into place and let her help him tighten the bolts. Within minutes, they finished the chore. She couldn't describe her feeling of euphoria. She had just learned to change a tire. Why did it have to be Mark Williams that made her feel this way? How could she still have feelings for this man?

"Thanks for teaching me what to do." She eyed her dirty fingers with a grimace.

"You're welcome."

Amazement filled her. Gone was the conceited athlete, replaced by a friendly, caring man. His hair fell into his eyes, his hands black with grime. A glaze of perspiration shadowed his face and neck, and stained the back of his shirt and underarms.

"It sure is hot today." Mark grinned as he placed the jack and flat tire in the trunk. "I think we're both gonna need to clean up after this."

She looked at her silk blouse and realized she also had rings of perspiration. Embarrassment heated her cheeks. She hated him to see her like this.

"I've got some wet wipes in the glove box." She hurried to reach into her car.

When she returned, he had closed the trunk and dusted off his hands. He smiled his thanks as he took several wipes and they both cleaned the majority of the grime from their hands.

She eyed the new tire, all ready for use. "I'd forgotten you were so good with cars."

He shrugged. "Back in high school, I could either repair them or walk, so I fixed the cars."

When he stepped back, she took a settling breath.

"Angie's gonna wonder what happened to me. I better get going."

"Yeah, me, too. Thanks again, Mark. I really appreciate it."

They each got into their own cars and he waited until she pulled onto the road. He followed her a short distance before he turned off to go retrieve Angie. It touched Emma deeply that he stayed close by long enough to ensure her car functioned properly. David would have sped away.

Somehow, things weren't the same anymore. Mark's presence in her life had rocked her world. It left her feeling insecure and shaky.

It left her wishing for things that could never be.

"Hi, Mrs. Perkins." Mark greeted Angie's child care provider. "Sorry I'm so late."

Mrs. Perkins held her front door open for him, a pleasant smile on her face. "Hi, Mark. Come on in."

As he stepped into her living room, the warm scent of something baking enveloped him and his stomach growled hungrily. He dreaded going home and trying to figure out what Angie might eat for dinner. Nothing seemed to appeal to her these days.

For just a moment he regretted not inviting Emma to dinner with him and Angie. He would have taken them out for Chinese or Mexican food. Anything but mac and cheese.

A quick scan of the cluttered room showed an absence of children. An umbrella stroller stood propped beside the wall of the entryway and various toys littered the green shag carpet.

Mark inhaled deeply. As usual, he was the last parent to pick up his child. He hated keeping Angie here so long, but Emma had needed him and he'd been glad to help her out.

"Angie, your father's here," Mrs. Perkins called.

As he followed her into the kitchen, he suffered a flicker of resentment when he thought of how Denise had abandoned them. As long as Mark lived, he would never understand why Denise had traded her family for a fling with a younger man. Deep in his heart, he would always mourn the death of his marriage.

Emma Shields filled his mind. Though he had just left her, he longed to see her again, just to talk and be near her. He couldn't help comparing Emma to Denise and discovered that he had put Emma on a high pedestal of strength, warmth and caring. It felt good to help her out after all she'd done for Angie.

Mrs. Perkins stood beside Angie at the kitchen table. Mark saw a plate of freshly baked cookies sitting there. Denise had never baked for Angie and he was grateful to Mrs. Perkins for the homey environment she offered his daughter. Another small blessing. God had been so kind, providing a way over every obstacle.

Now, if the tumor would just begin to shrink…

Angie leaned over a jigsaw puzzle spread across the tabletop. "Ah, do I hafta go right now? I'm almost done with my puzzle, Dad."

Moving to stand beside her, Mark looked down at the

puzzle showing fields of yellow daffodils and windmills. Only a handful of pieces were missing to complete the picture.

"Let her finish, Mark," Mrs. Perkins encouraged.

"Okay, hurry up. Then we'll get some dinner. I'm starving."

"Here, have some cookies," Mrs. Perkins urged, pushing the plate toward him.

He couldn't resist and took three cookies as Mrs. Perkins poured him a glass of milk.

"Thank you." He accepted the milk, then took a deep swallow.

Mrs. Perkins led the way back into the living room. "Come sit down and visit with me while you wait for Angie."

Mark followed and sat on the brown sectional sofa while she stooped to pick up toys and put them away. Now in her sixties and widowed, Mrs. Perkins showed energy uncommon in a woman her age.

"Thanks for all you do for Angie," Mark said. "I'm very grateful. She loves being here."

"It's my pleasure. She tells me you have a new girlfriend."

Mark almost choked on his milk and he tossed a glance toward Angie, who was happily unaware they were discussing her. "What?"

"She said it's that lady doctor you've been taking her to … Dr. Shields, I think? Angie said she likes her a lot."

"The doctor isn't my girlfriend. She's just Angie's oncologist."

Mrs. Perkins's brows lifted. "Oh? It sounds as if Angie thinks it's more than that."

"We knew each other when we were younger."

"Well, old friends can be the best. You already know if she has staying power."

It had been Mark that had broken off with Emma all those years ago. He had been the one to quit, not her. That gave him something to think about.

"I'm glad Angie likes her," Mrs. Perkins continued. "I haven't seen your daughter smile since Denise left, and now she's suddenly laughing and playing with the babies. Today, she tickled them. I've been wondering what the difference is and all I can figure is she's getting better, or it's Dr. Shields."

A knowing smile lit up Mrs. Perkins's face as she stood and went to gather up Angie's backpack, jacket and hat.

Later in the car, Mark steered with his left hand while he rubbed Angie's back with his right.

"How was your day?" he asked.

"Fine, but the babies kept crying. They drove me nuts!"

He laughed, delighted she'd had a busy day. "Angie, Mrs. Perkins said you mentioned Emma today."

Angie cast a quick glance at him, then shrugged. "Yeah, I told her about Sonja and the stickers she gives me, too."

"Do you...do you *like* Emma?"

"Of course, Dad. She's sad and all alone, just like us. She needs someone to love her. I need a new mommy and you need a new wife. Why not Emma?"

"Whoa, you're moving a bit fast for me, babe."

"When we know we've found the right mom, why should we wait?"

She saw things so simplistically. "What do you want for dinner?"

Staring out the passenger window, Angie shrugged. "I don't care."

Mark frowned. She used to love ice cream, pizza, burgers and every other type of fast food. Now, she didn't care if she ate anything.

"I think we've got some cheese and eggs at home. I need to go shopping tomorrow. Do you want to get a pizza tonight?"

"Okay." Her tone sounded dismal.

"I'll give you some Marinol as soon as we park the car. That should spark your appetite."

"Hey, this is Emma's neighborhood." Angie pointed down the street.

"Yeah, we're close to her house."

He'd driven clear across town to find a pizza shop.

Pulling into the lot at Big Ed's Pizza Shack, he parked the car and helped Angie out. Inside, he ordered an extra-large pizza with double cheese, then gave Angie her pills.

Angie stared over the counter as one of the workers pulled a pepperoni pizza from the oven. She sniffed the air and licked her lips. "That pepperoni sure looks good."

"Oh, I see how it is. If it's forbidden, *then* you're interested in eating. You know you can't eat pepperoni."

"I know, I know." Angie pouted. "But there's no harm if I smell it, is there?"

He laughed. "Of course not. I'd be willing to get you an ice-cream cone after dinner, if you want. Ice cream has lots of calcium in it."

Angie rolled her eyes. "Great! But just once, I'd like to eat something just because *I want to* and not because it's good for me, Dad."

He ignored her bad mood.

"You want to eat the pizza here?" he asked as he paid the bill.

The blue flowers bounced on her hat as she shook her head. "Nope, I want to eat it at Emma's house."

"We haven't been invited."

"So?" Angie said. "Why don't we invite Emma?"

Mark hesitated. "You think we should?"

"She's lonely, Dad. We should be friends with her."

If they showed up on Emma's doorstep, the worst she would say was, "No, go away."

"Come on." He picked up the pizza and took Angie's hand, then led her out to the car.

It was almost six in the evening and the summer sun still burned high and hot. Inside the car, Mark cranked up the air conditioner, then wiped his brow. He sure hoped Emma's house was cool.

They drove to Poole Avenue and parked in front of Emma's duplex. After he turned off the ignition, Mark clutched the steering wheel, hoping he wouldn't regret coming here.

He carried the pizza as they walked up to Emma's steps. Angie rang the doorbell and sweat broke out on his forehead.

"Please don't let this be a bad mistake," he mumbled beneath his breath.

Chapter Thirteen

Emma blew her nose and wiped her eyes, grateful to be dressed in a pair of cool capris and loose shirt. She had already removed her shoes and stood barefoot in the kitchen. It'd been a long day.

The doorbell rang and she made a hasty swipe of her face before she went to answer it.

"Mark!"

"Hi!" He smiled and hefted a pizza box. The tangy aroma of sauce and cheese wafted over her.

"What are you doing here?"

Angie stood beside him, showing a gape-toothed grin where she'd lost another baby tooth. "Hi, Emma!"

She couldn't help smiling at the child. "Hi! I see you've lost another tooth. It isn't a permanent tooth, is it?"

Emma glanced at Mark.

"No, it's a baby tooth. I remembered you said the chemo is hard on teeth, so I give her the calcium supplements you suggested and make sure she brushes."

"Good," Emma responded. "So what can I do for you?" She wondered why they were here.

Mark inclined his head, his eyes sparkling as he smiled. “We were in the neighborhood and just picked up an extra-large cheese pizza. Care to share it with us?”

She hesitated for several moments.

“I, uh, well—okay, come in.” Stepping back, she let them enter, watching Mark’s gaze sweep over her open floor plan that allowed her to see from the small living room to the kitchen and backyard.

She was suddenly conscious of her plain decor, the beige couch and love seat and drab brown carpet that ended where the linoleum of the kitchen started. The furniture had come with the duplex and she’d seen no reason to change anything. She had bought the place, intending to keep it as a rental once she got a house. That had been two years ago and she hadn’t moved yet.

Pictures of Brian hung from the walls and sat atop the piano, which she hadn’t played since her son died. A single vase of dried field flowers rested beside the front door. Otherwise, the room looked as austere and cold as her heart.

“Nice apartment.” Mark glanced at the pictures of Brian at various ages.

She saw that he was curious about the boy, but he didn’t ask, thank goodness. Instead, he sniffed the air.

“You’re baking cookies!” Angie cried.

Mark’s eyes widened with amazement. “You’re baking, too?”

“Too?” Emma asked.

“Uh, Mrs. Perkins was baking cookies today.”

“Oh.” Emma wiped her nose with a tissue. Brian had loved her chocolate-chip cookies. Since it was his birthday today, she was feeling wistful and needed something to keep her mind busy.

Mark's gaze swept her from head to toe and his eyes twinkled with approval. A smile as wide as Kansas spread across his face.

Something went soft and mellow inside her chest. Her thoughts scattered and she wondered vaguely how she could fight his charm.

Looking down at herself, she noticed her apron was covered with flour and she dusted it off. She wriggled her toes, wishing he hadn't caught her looking less than her best.

"Angie, how are you feeling today?" she asked.

Angie stepped to the edge of the carpet and peaked into the kitchen, then craned her head toward the stove. Lifting her nose, she sniffed, testing the air.

"I'm fine, thank you," Angie replied in an exuberant tone. "Are the cookies ready yet?"

Emma laughed. The child's eagerness touched a soft chord within her. Brian would have wolfed half of them down by now.

"Yes, help yourself. There's plenty cooling on the counter and I've got the last batch in the oven."

"Yay!" Angie attacked the cooling rack.

"Only one for now," Mark called. "You don't want to ruin your dinner."

"Ah!" came Angie's muffled reply. She had already stuffed an entire cookie into her mouth.

Shaking his head and chuckling, Mark walked to the kitchen table and set the pizza down. "I'm sorry, Emma. I didn't know she would react this way. She seems so happy whenever we see you. Denise never—uh, there aren't too many people that make us cookies."

Us.

It had been too long since she had been an "us." Did he assume she had made the cookies for them? She rather liked the idea of trying out new recipes on Mark and Angie.

"It's okay. I didn't know what to do with so many cookies anyway."

Emma's gaze locked with Mark's and she shifted nervously, conscious of the sounds of Angie munching on her chocolate-chip cookie. Somehow, it was just what Emma wanted. To share her cookies with a sweet little girl and her handsome father.

Sitting on the cream-colored sofa, Mark leaned back and draped his arms along the back. The movement was completely male and stretched his shirt taut across his broad shoulders and chest. The rich color of his burgundy shirt added vibrant contrast to the room.

He adds color to my life.

"She has an appetite today. I guess the Marinol is working, huh?" she asked.

"Yeah, I guess it is." Mark shifted and crossed his legs.

He's as edgy as I am.

"Mmm, great cookies, Emma." Dusting off her hands, Angie came into the living room and sat beside her father. She kicked off her sandals and scooted her bottom back against the couch, then curled her legs beneath her. She seemed very much at home.

"May I watch the news?" Angie asked politely.

News? Emma blinked as she went to switch the television on. "Sure."

"Thanks for the reminder, Angie," Mark exclaimed. "We're going to be on the six o'clock news tonight."

"They interviewed Dad and me for Make-A-Wish."

Emma glanced at the anniversary clock sitting on the mantel. "Well, ten more minutes and we'll get to see it."

She went to the cabinet where her VCR was kept and pulled out a blank cassette. "How about if I record it for you?"

"Thanks, Emma. I didn't think about that, but it might be fun," Mark agreed.

She pressed the on button to the VCR and programmed the machine to record the news program. As she passed Angie on her way back to the kitchen, she reached out and caressed the girl's arm.

Looking up, Emma caught Mark studying her. She pulled her hand away from Angie and stumbled backward.

"Whoa! Are you okay?" Mark sat forward on the sofa.

"Yeah, I'm just a bit clumsy."

"Have you been crying?" Angie asked.

Emma wiped her nose and headed toward the kitchen. "Uhm, no, why do you ask?"

"Your eyes are red and your nose is drippy."

"Angie!" Mark spoke up. "Don't be rude."

Observant little imp. Emma was *not* about to confess she'd spent an hour visiting Brian's grave this afternoon. Then, to make her feel even better, her ex-husband's sister had just called to inform her David had remarried last week and was now honeymooning in the Caribbean. Though Emma no longer loved him, it still hurt.

"I have a bad cold," she said.

Angie hopped off the couch. Mark followed as Angie walked to the kitchen table where a small square cake sat. Seven candles protruded from the white frosting with the words "Happy Birthday, Brian" written across the top in dark blue icing.

"Oh, I need to clean up this mess—" Emma whisked the cake off the table and popped it into the refrigerator, out of sight.

"Who's Brian?" Angie asked.

Heat crept over Emma's face as Mark's gaze followed her. "He…he was my son."

Mark's eyes widened. "Your son?"

"I didn't know you had a son," Angie said. "Where is he?"

Emma bit her bottom lip. She wasn't ready for this. Thankfully the timer rang, warning that the cookies were done.

"Emma, we didn't mean to intrude if this is a bad time for you," Mark said. "Maybe we should go."

"No, please stay." She took the last batch out of the oven, then flipped the temperature onto warm and popped the pizza in until they were ready to eat.

She didn't want to be alone. Not tonight.

"Hey, the news is on." Angie raced back to the couch.

Grateful for the distraction, Emma breathed with relief. She joined Mark and Angie on the couch and listened to reports on a sales tax increase, a new home development coming into the city, a nuclear explosion in Kiev and other top stories.

Finally the piece on donating frequent flyer miles to Make-A-Wish was announced and Mark appeared on the screen dressed in a navy suit and yellow tie.

"Dad, that's you!" Angie squealed at the TV, where he was being interviewed by Nikki Colfax of Channel 6 News.

"I know. Shh, let's listen," he said to quiet her.

Mark spoke briefly about the Make-A-Wish program

and charitable donations. Then the camera showed him walking hand-in-hand with Angie down a sidewalk in front of her school.

Nikki Colfax's voice accompanied the presentation. "At some point, doctors believe his daughter will succumb to the brain tumor she was diagnosed with nine months ago. That means the seven days Mark Williams will spend with his daughter at Disney World will be a dream come true."

Mark stared at the screen, his eyes wide with shock. So did Emma.

Nikki's voice continued. "The program is called Miles for Kids in Need and you can donate all the miles you've saved up to give a critically ill child a dream vacation. Even your miles that are about to expire can be used by the charity. If you'd like to donate miles, call the number on your screen and make a difference in a child's life."

Angie looked between Emma and Mark. "Dad, what does *succumb* mean?"

All the blood seemed to drain from Mark's face. In that moment Emma realized he was as stunned as she was that Nikki Colfax had said Angie would succumb to her illness.

"It means to defeat," Emma answered before he could respond. "It means you're going to beat this brain tumor, Angie, and don't you ever let anyone tell you anything different."

Emma had half a mind to call the news station and give that reporter a piece of her mind.

Angie grinned. "That's right. I'm gonna beat it." The girl lifted her arms in the air and pranced around the living room chanting, "I'm gonna beat it. I'm gonna beat it."

Mark interrupted the child by swinging her up in his arms and blowing raspberries on her neck. She squealed and squirmed until he put her down. Then, she wiped the wetness off her skin and threw him a look of disgust. "Yuck, Dad, you slobbered all over me."

His deep laughter rang throughout the house and Emma couldn't help smiling.

"Hey, are you gonna help me with dinner?" Emma asked.

She stood and took Angie by the hand, leaving Mark to stare after them.

Before long, he joined them at the sink and the three worked side by side as Mark set the table while Angie helped Emma toss a green salad and slice fresh fruit. Emma got a stool for Angie, and the girl kept up a nonstop stream of chatter as she rinsed lettuce leaves and tomatoes.

"Mom never let me help cook," Angie said. "She was afraid I'd make a mess. Of course, Mom only knows how to make hot dogs and mac and cheese."

Emma didn't respond, but she sensed sadness in the child's words.

Mark dipped his fingers into the water and flicked drops at Angie and Emma. "Well, *we* don't mind a little mess, do we?"

"Definitely not." Emma flipped droplets of water back at him.

"Hey, you got me wet!" Angie yelled, and splashed her father.

Emma grabbed her squirt bottle from the linen closet and let Mark have a spritz right in the face. As he blinked and wiped his chin, a devilish light filled his eyes and he came after her. Her shrill scream mingled with his chuckles as he chased her around the table with Angie close on his heels.

He caught Emma on the other side, tickling her ribs as Angie wrapped her arms around him for a tight squeeze. Their hilarity and shouts filled the kitchen.

Finally they settled down, all of them dripping. The smile slid off Emma's face as she got them each a dish towel to dry off with.

As she returned to the sink to finish washing the cucumbers, Emma realized this was what she longed for: a kind man and children laughing in her kitchen while she fixed them dinner.

At Emma's urging, Angie placed a bowl of roses from Emma's garden in the center of the table and Emma took the opportunity to speak quietly with Mark.

"Mark, I'm sorry if I said something I shouldn't have about the news program. As Angie's doctor, I just didn't think it was good for her health or morale to hear someone say she was going to succumb to her illness."

He shook his head and whispered back, "No, thank you for being so quick. I was dumbfounded. At no time during the interview did I *ever* tell Nikki Colfax that Angie might die. Even if it were true, I would never, ever, tell a stranger that, especially knowing Angie might hear it."

Emma shrugged. "You know reporters. Most are only interested in padding the drama of their news for higher ratings. They don't stop to consider who they might hurt in the process."

"Yeah, well, I won't do another interview like that with Angie again. But I may have a problem later when she tries to convince one of her schoolteachers that succumb means to defeat."

Emma chuckled and observed the smiling child as she folded paper napkins by each of their plates. "She feels good today."

Mark nodded. "She always feels good when we spend time with you. She eats better, too."

His words sent a flock of butterflies to Emma's stomach. As she set a bottle of salad dressing on the table, she bumped against Mark and he reached to steady her. Their gazes locked and she found herself drowning in the green depths of his eyes.

"Are you hungry?" His smile dazzled her.

"Definitely." She stepped back. "Come on, Angie. Let's eat."

They gathered around the table. When Mark bowed his head Emma and Angie followed suit. Mark asked a quick blessing on the food, thanking God for their lives and for Emma's help to kill the tumor. Then he and Angie dug in.

Looking down at her cheese pizza and salad, Emma felt ashamed. All she had ever done was ask God for things or complain because He hadn't done enough. When was the last time she had given Him thanks for all the blessings in her life?

She couldn't remember.

She had everything she could possibly need, except what she really wanted. And yet she was thankful to have been Brian's mother. How enriched her life was because of him. Maybe later on, when she was alone, she should tell God that.

"Don't you think so, Emma?"

She looked up and found Mark staring at her. "I'm sorry, I didn't hear—"

"Look! There's a kitty," Angie shouted.

The girl scooted back from the table and ran to the sliding glass door where an orange tabby sat swishing its tail on the back step. The cat meowed and nudged the glass pane with its black nose.

"That's my neighbor's cat, Wilbur," Emma supplied. "He comes over here looking for food and hoping I'll pet him."

Angie hunkered down by the door and rubbed her finger against the glass. "Can he come in?"

Emma shook her head. "Nope, sorry, I'm allergic. You can go out into the backyard and play with him, though."

Sliding the glass door open, Emma allowed Angie to slip through to the back deck.

"Do you need me to come with you?" Mark asked.

"No, Dad," Angie snapped. "I think I can play by myself."

The girl scooped up the cat, rubbing her face against the animal's soft fur.

Mark's eyes widened at her surly tone. "I guess she's extra tired today."

Emma bit her tongue. Angie didn't act tired. She acted annoyed by her father. Though Emma thought Mark was too protective of his daughter, it wasn't her place to criticize him.

"She won't catch any disease from the cat, will she?" Mark looked anxious. "I know her immune system isn't strong right now."

"She'll be fine, Mark," Emma said.

Definitely overly protective, yet Emma couldn't blame him.

She left the sliding door open just a crack, so they

could hear Angie if she called out. Even from this distance, they could see the girl and hear her delighted giggles and Wilbur's purrs as Angie scratched his ears.

When Angie took the cat over to sit on the grass, Mark started to rise from his chair. Emma stopped him with a lift of her hand. "She's fine, Mark. It's a nice, safe, fenced yard. Let her play for a while."

He sat back down but his gaze followed Angie for several more minutes and silence loomed throughout the room.

"She thinks I'm domineering and pushy." Mark shrugged. "But I just want what's best for her."

"I know. When you're fighting to save someone's life, it's hard to think about anything else." Emma spoke without humor.

He gazed into her eyes. "You talk as though you know what it's like, Emma."

She moved her gaze to Angie. If she told him about Brian, it would only make things more difficult. It didn't help when he reached across the table and squeezed her hand gently.

Knots of tension cramped her stomach. She stared at their entwined fingers, feeling guilty for enjoying the touch of this warm, attractive man.

She jerked her hand back. "Don't."

He looked hurt and Emma refused to meet his eyes.

"Don't you think it's time you told me what happened to your son, Emmy?" he said.

Emma froze, feeling as though a guillotine had chopped off her windpipe.

Chapter Fourteen

"I don't like being called Emmy," Emma said, ignoring Mark's question about Brian.

Mark's brow furrowed in confusion. "But I've called you that name ever since first grade."

Glancing across the kitchen table, her gaze meshed with his. Images of David flashed through her mind. The last time she had seen David, his eyes had been filled with hate as he shouted that she had murdered their son. Even now, the memory chilled her blood.

Mark's eyes filled with hope and had the power to melt her frozen heart.

She reached for the salt shaker, rubbing it between her palms in a nervous gesture. A lump formed in her throat but she managed to speak around it. "I know you've always called me Emmy, but it's just that—"

She wanted to explain about Brian's death, but the words stuck in her throat.

"Emma, what's wrong? You can trust me."

Every fiber of her being responded to his gentle urging and she heaved a weary sigh. "David called me

Emmy when he—" Her voice cracked and she tried again. "When he blamed me for our son's death."

Mark rubbed his fingertips against his forehead. "Oh, boy. I'm sorry. I didn't mean to pry. I feel like such a heel."

"It's not your fault."

"You know you'll see him again, right?" Mark added.

"David?"

He shook his head. "No, Brian. Your son."

Something cold gripped her. "I don't believe in eternity, Mark."

She didn't mean it. Not really. But the anger and hurt she kept bottled up inside ever since Brian died seemed to rise to the surface now. Mark was the first person she had confided in.

"You don't mean that, Emma."

Oh, he knew her so well.

How desperately she wanted to believe she would see Brian again.

She thought about what Mark said, knowing in her heart it was true. Yet her personal guilt and regret over her son's death kept her from admitting it.

He clasped his fingers around hers and she couldn't pull away.

"I want us to be friends," he said.

Warmth tingled up her arm. She should let go.

She held on tighter. He filled the emptiness in her life, but he had his daughter to think about. He didn't need a neurotic woman grieving for her son to muddy up his life.

She let go of his hand.

"Do you still like to go fishing?" Mark asked.

She burst out laughing, his question completely unexpected. "Yes, but I haven't gone since—"

The summer before their junior year in high school, Emma had gone fishing with Mark. Brett and Tina and one other couple from school joined them and they'd laughed and shared a picnic of fried chicken, potato salad and s'mores. Mark had helped her land her first trout, teasing her because it was so puny. They'd thrown the fish back and splashed each other and played until the sun went down. That evening, when Mark had dropped her off at her doorstep, he'd kissed her.

Her first kiss. And it had been magic.

Now they exchanged a secret smile and Mark lifted a hand to brush his knuckles against her hair. "You remember, too?"

"Yes, one of the best memories of my life."

"I've never been anyone's best memory, Emma." His smile faded. "There are times when I wish Denise and I could go back to the way things were, before the divorce. I keep thinking I could change things somehow, if only I had a second chance."

A muscle ticked in his lean cheek and his gaze was filled with so much pain. Mark Williams wasn't as one-dimensional as she had thought.

"I shouldn't have told you that," he said. "But you're much more to me than just Angie's doctor."

"Mark, I'm sorry about Denise. I wish we hadn't brought up such sad memories."

"It's not your fault."

A stilted silence followed. She longed to confide in him, to be his friend and much more, but doubt filled her mind. She had trusted David, but he'd turned his back on her long before Brian died.

"Mark, I know what it's like to watch your child

waste away and die from cancer. It would kill me to go through that again. I just couldn't do it a second time."

She could tell from his expression he understood what she was saying. She didn't want to be Angie's surrogate mother. And yet, in many ways, it was already too late. She loved his little girl. If the worst happened, Emma knew her heart would be shattered once more.

His cell phone started ringing and he scrambled to pull it from his pants' pocket. Emma breathed a sigh of relief for the interruption.

"Hello?"

His smile dropped like stone.

"Denise! It's been weeks since we heard from you—"

He paused, listening.

"Oh, you saw the news program, huh? Yeah, Angie's here. Wait and I'll get her for you— What? Yes, I received the forms yesterday in the mail."

Emma looked away, embarrassed to be listening to his private conversation. She stood and moved to the living room, where she picked up a pile of magazines and began to sort through them. She could see Mark's profile as he leaned against the counter in her kitchen, trying to speak softly to his ex-wife.

"No, I haven't had time, but I'll mail them back to you on Monday." Another pause and his shoulders stiffened. "I can't do that. I'm with Angie now."

Tension pulsed from him, so thick Emma could have sliced it with a cleaver. "No, tomorrow is Saturday and I'm not taking Angie to Mrs. Perkins. She spends enough time away from home as it is. Now, if you'll hold a moment, I'll get her for you—"

With the phone pressed to his ear, he stepped toward

the glass door but hesitated, his features hard. "But she asks for you every day. Why can't you talk to her for a few minutes?"

Pinching the bridge of his nose, he clenched his jaw. "Yeah, yeah, I understand perfectly."

How could Denise be so cruel?

"Okay." Mark spoke in a resigned tone. "Do what you want."

He hung up the phone and pocketed it, staring out the sliding-glass door at Angie, his legs spread slightly as he lifted his hands to his hips and heaved a deep huff of air. It was a masculine stance, exposing his pensive thoughts.

Oblivious that her mother had just been on the phone and didn't want to talk to her, Angie continued to stroke the cat. The sweet expression on her face as she smiled and talked softly to Wilbur was so innocent and genuine that Emma felt a poignant sense of loss.

Mark faced Emma. His features softened and he seemed to relax. "I'm sorry you had to hear that."

Emma wished she could say something to lessen the sting. "I'm sorry, too. You and Angie shouldn't have to go through this, and I can't tell you how much I admire your strength. You're such a great example to me."

In unison, they stared at the girl as Wilbur sprawled on his back in the grass and Angie rubbed his furry tummy.

"She's happy and confident in your love," Emma said.

He came to stand beside Emma and took her hand in his. "Sometimes when I see Angie so sick and I talk to Denise, I wonder if I'm fooling myself. Maybe God has forsaken us. Maybe I'm wrong and—"

Emma wrenched her hand free. Tears blurred her

vision. "Don't say that. I want so desperately to hope, to have faith. If *you* doubt, then I fear there's no hope for me."

He gave a shuddering laugh and scrubbed a hand against his jaw. "You're right. How can I doubt when I witness the miracle you bring into my life? I must sound ungrateful, when I have so much to be thankful for. Thanks for bringing me back to my senses."

He peered at the backyard and smiled when Angie dangled a blade of grass over Wilbur's head. The cat batted it with his front paws.

"The divorce was my fault," he said. "I worked too much and built our lives around material things. I should've been home more. I should've told Denise I loved her. It might have helped."

"Now, you're making excuses for Denise."

Anguish flashed across his face. "I know, but I can't help wishing I'd done more."

"I'm the same. I was too wrapped up in trying to save my son's life to work out the problems in my marriage."

Mark leaned against the wall and folded his arms. "I do know there's no hurt, emotional or physical, that the Savior hasn't already felt. The Atonement isn't just for sinners, Emma. It also heals carelessness, inadequacy and bitterness. Without it, our lives would be utterly meaningless."

His words touched her. "Still trying to convert me?"

He shrugged. "Let's just say we *all* need reminding on a regular basis."

She perched herself on the arm of the sofa. "We are an odd pair, aren't we?"

As he stepped near and gave her a quick hug, she tensed, liking the comfort he offered, yet worried it wasn't a lasting thing. "I like the sound of that. There's no one I'd rather be with, Emma."

She stood and sidled away, her nerves clenching. By encouraging Mark, she only opened herself up to more complications. Being friends was one thing, but this was much more.

"It's okay to talk about him, you know," Mark said.

She didn't pretend not to understand. "It hurts too much to talk about Brian."

"I know. I don't usually talk much about Denise, but maybe we both need a safe outlet where what we say doesn't go anywhere else."

It was a revelation to realize she wasn't the only one with regrets in her life. If what Mark said was true, the Atonement could swallow her pain. She could turn her remorse and guilt over to God. Asking the Lord to take it from her shoulders seemed so easy, yet she didn't know if she could relinquish control that way.

He released a breath of air. "Thanks for letting me talk. I can't tell you how much I needed it."

A hard lump formed in her throat and she tried to swallow. There was no getting away from the heartache tucked inside her soul. And yet, by sharing her burden with Mark, it didn't feel quite so heavy anymore. "You're welcome."

Emma's heart was filled with so many doubts. Maybe prayer was the key. Later tonight, she could try it. If it didn't work, no harm done.

She gazed at Angie. The sun glinted off the child's smiling face as she chased Wilbur across the yard. The cat climbed the wooden fence and disappeared.

"Here, kitty, kitty, kitty," Angie trilled.

She called over and over, but Wilbur didn't return.

"It's not your fault, you know," Mark said.

Emma's shoulders stiffened. "What?"

His voice lowered. "That Brian died. He wouldn't want you unhappy."

"How do you know I'm unhappy?"

"I have eyes in my head, Emma. And Sonja mentioned that—"

"Sonja! Look, Mark, I really wish you'd stop listening to her. I'm a big girl and can take care of myself."

"I'm sorry."

He had crossed the line. She wished people would leave her alone. The more she thought of Sonja, Larry Meacham and Mark meddling in her life, the angrier she became.

"My personal life is none of your business," she told him.

"Emma, don't."

"This was a mistake, Mark. I should never have invited you in. I think you should go." She started to clear the table, conscious of him hovering nearby.

"Emma, I didn't mean to hurt you."

She didn't respond. His presence was magnetic, his voice so sincere and inviting. Like a haven from heaven. All she had to do was reach out and—

She kept moving, rinsing plates before putting them in the dishwasher, covering the salad bowl with plastic wrap and popping it into the refrigerator. Her movements were stiff and erratic. The companionship she had enjoyed with him evaporated.

Mark stepped close and her stomach churned into tight little knots. "Emma, please forgive me."

Mark apologizing? He really had changed, but it was too late for them.

"There's nothing to forgive." She moved past him, avoiding his eyes. "I'll see you tomorrow night at the Make-A-Wish meeting. Thanks for coming by."

She leaned against the counter, folded her arms and stared out the window. It was a sharp invitation for him to leave.

With a deep sigh, he stepped to the glass door and called to Angie. Emma almost breathed a sigh of relief.

Angie came inside like a little tornado, so full of life, so happy. The difference was amazing.

"Oh, I love Wilbur, Daddy. Can we get a kitty, please, please, please?" She hopped up and down. "I want a yellow one and I'll name him Tiger."

Emma had never seen Angie this animated. The child had just received a chemo injection three days ago, so she should be feeling sluggish. Surely a plate of chocolate-chip cookies, a slice of pizza and a cat named Wilbur couldn't make the difference.

Angie raced over to throw her arms around Emma's waist for a tight squeeze. "I had so much fun. Can I come over and play with your kitty tomorrow?"

Waves of emotion washed over Emma and she squeezed her eyes shut, resisting the urge to hug the girl back.

"He's not my cat." Emma spoke around the lump clogging her throat.

"Can we come visit you anyway?"

It was no use. Emma couldn't resist. None of this wretched situation was Angie's fault.

Cupping the girl's cheek with her palm, Emma stared

down into her sparkling eyes. "I'm sure Wilbur would like that, sweetheart."

Looking delighted by Emma's response, Angie clasped her father's hand.

"Thanks for a wonderful evening, Emma." Mark led Angie to the front door.

"You're welcome." Her voice sounded tight and she didn't see them to the door.

She walked to the living room and pushed back the lace curtains to stare out the small window. As she watched them drive down the street, she felt numb and empty inside.

Chapter Fifteen

"Good morning," Mark greeted Darcy the following week.

Standing at the front reception counter, he smiled as he signed in for Angie's appointment.

Angie stood on tiptoe as she peeped over the counter. "Hi, Darcy."

"Hi, cutie. How are you?" Darcy smiled with affection as she tugged playfully on the brim of Angie's baseball cap.

"Fine." Angie's voice sounded buoyant.

Mark glanced around the reception room. "Mrs. Valdez isn't here yet?"

After two months Angie had become quite attached to Mrs. Valdez.

Darcy showed a hesitant frown. "No, I'm sorry, but she won't be here. Mrs. Valdez died."

Angie gasped, her eyes flashing wide.

"Died? When?" Mark said.

"Well, I, um, I'm not sure—"

"No." Angie gave a small whimper and backed away

from the counter, shaking her head. Tears filled her eyes and her little chin quivered.

"Angie—" Mark stepped toward her, his arms outstretched.

"No! It's not true," she yelled, and took off through the office, sprinting toward the treatment room.

"Mrs. Valdez! Mrs. Valdez!" Angie yelled, circling around the hallway with Mark in hot pursuit.

Her cries filled the entire office and brought several staff members running. They stared in confusion as Angie made her second pass through the hall. Angie spied Emma standing at the end of the corridor. The girl made a beeline toward the doctor and threw her arms around Emma's legs.

Holding tight, the child pressed her face against Emma's abdomen, sobbing. "She's not dead, she's not. You can make her better, Emma. You can bring her back, can't you? Please, please bring her back."

Staring down at Angie, Emma's eyes went wide with surprise. She held her hands up, as if she didn't know quite what to do.

Mark dropped down on his knees beside his daughter, trying to comfort her. He tried to take Angie into his arms, but she shook him off, clinging to Emma.

"No, let me be," Angie cried. "Emma, please."

Mark glanced up at Emma and saw her confusion. She knelt in front of Angie and pulled the girl into her arms.

"What happened?" Emma asked over the top of Angie's head.

"She just found out Mrs. Valdez died. Why didn't you warn me so I could have prepared her?" he asked.

Tears flickered in Emma's eyes, her expression one

of helplessness. "I only found out half an hour ago. I didn't realize Angie would take it this hard or I would have called you."

Mark hadn't realized, either. First her mother, now Mrs. Valdez. He should have talked with Angie about this possibility; he should have prepared her for it.

"No, she's not dead, she's not!" Angie's words were muffled against Emma's neck.

"Angie, listen to me." Mark tried to pry her away, but Angie clung tighter to Emma.

"No, I want Emma." The child wept, her pitiful sobs filling the office. The staff members stood around staring, their faces white with shock.

All this time, Mark had been worried about becoming romantically attached to Emma, it never occurred to him that Angie might become too attached to her, as well. Maybe he had done his daughter a disservice by spending time with Emma. Eventually she would leave them, just like Denise. When that time came, it would devastate his daughter.

"Angie." Emma spoke against the girl's ear, soft and soothing. "Listen to me, sweetie. Mrs. Valdez was very old and very sick, but she lived a long, happy life. Her husband was with her right up to the end and she passed away quietly without pain."

The sobbing subsided into hiccups as Angie listened intently, her tear-drenched face pressed against Emma's cheek.

"I know we'll all miss her," Emma continued, "but there was nothing we could do to help her and it would have been cruel to make her stay with us any longer. She's at peace now."

Rubbing her eyes, Angie gave a little shudder as she drew back and looked at Emma, their noses barely touching. "Am I gonna die, too?"

The words chopped off Mark's words, thoughts and heartbeat.

It was the first time Angie asked this question out loud. He had wondered if she was too young to understand the ramifications of her brain tumor, but she was smart and insightful and he should have known better. He had tried to keep her morale positive but should have addressed her fears better.

"No!" Emma answered fiercely, hugging Angie close. "No, sweetie. I won't let you. Mrs. Valdez had a deadly cancer that you don't have. You mustn't give up hope. Your dad and I will do everything in our power to keep you safe. I promise you."

Mark gave a weak smile, approving of what Emma said. He refused to give up. Angie needed to know that.

"Emma's right, honey." He caressed Angie's cheek, his heart aching. "We're never going to give up this fight. Never."

The sounds of the office filtered over them, the ringing of the phone, the buzz of machinery and voices coming from the reception room.

Angie looked into Emma's eyes. "Are you gonna leave Dad and me, like Mommy and Mrs. Valdez?"

Emma glanced at Mark, then hugged Angie tight. "No, I'll always be here for as long as you want me."

She meant what she said. Every single word. If she had to call in every favor of every medical professional she knew, she vowed she would not let this child die as long as she could do something to prevent it.

Please, God! Please let me keep my promise. Please help me have faith, to be strong for Angie and Mark.

Emma didn't resist the burn of tears. She was so overcome by emotion, she just didn't have the strength or desire to fight it any longer.

Over the top of Angie's head, Emma saw Mark's face contort with emotion. A single tear tumbled down his cheek and Emma could hardly stand to see this strong man cry.

He wiped at his right eye and inhaled a deep breath before he let it out in a fast exhale. "Thanks, Emma."

Knowing he depended on her brought Emma a hot gush of achy pleasure. And yet, it scared her to death. Old fears of failure crowded her mind. If the new chemo protocol Emma had discussed with Larry Meacham didn't work—

She couldn't think about that now. God had given her that insight and she mustn't doubt it.

They walked into the treatment room where Emma stayed with Angie while Sonja administered the chemo injection. By the time Mark led his daughter out of the office, Angie was calm and smiling once more.

When they were gone, Emma went into her office and closed the door. Sitting all alone, she contemplated this turn of events. And then, she did something she had longed to do but hadn't done in years.

She lowered herself to her knees beside the mahogany desk and bowed her head. Clasping her hands tightly in her lap, she closed her eyes and started to pray. She offered her gratitude for all her blessings, and for Mark and Angie bringing such sweetness into her life. Every careworn fear and hurt poured out of her as she expressed her deepest desires to her Heavenly Father.

When she finished speaking, she felt a divine peace resting upon her like the summer sun after a harsh winter storm.

As she went to the restroom and rinsed her face, she stopped trying to understand the calm that filled her soul. God loved her, she knew that now with every fiber of her being. And for the first time since Brian's death, she no longer felt alone.

Chapter Sixteen

The day of the Make-A-Wish barbecue started out hot and dry. Emma showered and dressed in short overalls and a robin's-egg blue top before she applied her makeup. She couldn't decide whether she should pull her long hair up in a clip and enjoy a cooling breeze against her neck or curl her hair and wear it down around her face. There had been times when she noticed Mark's appreciative gaze resting on her long hair and she knew instinctively that he preferred it down.

Vanity did ugly things to a woman's comfort.

She left it down, curling, primping, spraying until it was almost time for Mark to pick her up. They had to arrive at the park early so they could set up their hamburger/hot dog stand and have everything in order for the crowds.

With one last spritz of cologne, she went out into her living room and gathered up her keys and purse. The doorbell rang and she hurried to open it, her heart thumping with excitement.

"Hi, Emma!" Angie grinned.

Emma smiled and squeezed Angie's shoulder as she hunkered down so she could look the girl in the eyes. "Hasn't that new tooth come in yet?"

Angie shook her head, the flowers on her hat jiggling. "Nope. And I lost another one back here."

The girl opened her mouth wider to show Emma the gap in her teeth.

"Ah, I see. And did the tooth fairy bring you something for that?" Emma asked.

"Yeah, a whole dollar." Angie smiled and scuffed her sandaled foot against the door mat.

Emma peered over Angie's head. Mark stood beside his truck, a slow grin spreading across his face, his hands slung low in the pockets of his denim jeans. Now, this was a change, letting Angie come to get Emma alone. Maybe Mark was loosening up a bit.

"Well, I'm ready." Emma stepped out onto the front steps and pulled the door closed behind her.

As they walked across the lawn, Angie reached out and took Emma's hand, hopping along, chattering about the fun they were going to have at the barbecue.

"There's gonna be food, games and a three-legged race." Her nose wrinkled with repugnance. "But they're gonna play fifties music."

Emma's brows quirked. "You don't like fifties music?"

"Nah," she shook her head. "Too old-fashioned. Did you know Dad volunteered for the dunking booth?"

Lifting her head, Emma's gaze locked with Mark's as he rounded the Silverado and came to open the door for her. He'd shaved, his lean jaw strong and masculine.

"Hi, there." He greeted her with a smile.

His nearness caused her pulse to race.

"Hi. You volunteered for the dunking booth, huh?" Emma tossed him a speculative smile.

His grin widened and she knew from his expression that he had read her mind.

"Don't even think about it, Emma Shields," he warned with a chuckle.

"What?" she asked in an innocent tone.

"I know what you have in mind." Deep laughter rumbled in his chest as he closed her door and rounded the truck to the driver's side.

"Did you bring some extra towels?" she asked when he got inside.

He reached to help Angie buckle her seat belt. "I've got one."

"Good. You're gonna need it." She smirked.

He chuckled. "I remember your throwing arm from high school and, trust me, lady, it was lousy."

She burst out laughing. "True, I was always too busy with geometry and biology to go out for any sports. But I think my throwing arm has improved since then."

"Maybe next weekend we can take Angie to the park to play some baseball." He gave an exaggerated lift of his brows. "You *do* still like baseball, don't you?"

A memory of him chasing her around the bases when they were in high school overwhelmed her and she felt a heated flush stain her cheeks. She stared out the window at the passing traffic. Another vision filled her mind, of Brian dressed in his Little League uniform, running the bases, the exhilaration of victory on his face as he scored his first home run. Instead of causing her pain, the memory warmed her heart.

Was this the peace of God?

"I don't mind baseball at all. In fact, it's my favorite sport," she told Mark.

He flashed her a smile of approval. "Mine, too."

When they arrived at the park, they set to work, unloading paper goods, buns and coolers containing hamburger patties and hot dogs from the back of Mark's truck. Angie pitched in, carrying bags of foam cups.

Concession booths with white canopies were already set up all over the park. Soon they would be filled with food, games and activities for young and old to enjoy.

One of the Make-A-Wish volunteers chaperoned Angie and a group of other Wish Kids to play games while Mark and Emma ran the hamburger booth. Wearing a long, white apron, Mark flipped burgers while Emma took orders.

A voice over the loudspeaker announced each event and starting whistles and horns filled the air. Heat sweltered near the grill and, before long, sweat poured off Emma's face. She pushed her long hair away from her neck, finding it slightly damp. No doubt it had lost its curl and would be straight as spaghetti. So much for trying to look nice for Mark. Hopefully he wouldn't notice her disheveled appearance.

"I think I'm going to enjoy that dunking booth after this." He wiped his forehead with his shirt sleeve.

Emma reached past him for another case of buns. As she lifted the heavy box, she tottered and found the load suddenly removed from her arms as Mark took it and set it aside.

"These boxes are too heavy for you to lift, Emma. Let me get them."

"Thank you," she said.

He grinned as he salted the burger patties. In the close confines of the booth, they found a rhythm, working together side by side.

"Two more burgers and a dog," Emma called.

"Coming right up!" Mark returned.

Happy laughter from the crowd filtered over them, the hum of fifties music floating on the air. Mark began to sing along, flipping burgers on the grill like an expert. As she watched him work, something deep inside Emma melted. And right there, standing in the middle of the hamburger booth, clutching a hot dog bun in one hand, with ketchup on her elbow, lightning struck Emma's heart.

She wanted to see Mark every day, to talk to him, to hear his voice and to know he was there for her. The thought of not seeing him and Angie after the girl finished her treatments brought a sickening dread to Emma's chest.

It had happened. She had fallen in love. Now that her heart was committed, she faced the horrific pain of losing someone she cared deeply about.

Again.

And yet, it no longer brought her fear. Staring across the booth at Mark, she watched as he popped patties onto buns, a wide smile on his face, his voice filled with happiness as he tossed three more raw burgers on the grill.

"You want those with grilled onions?" he called to a burly man with a bald head.

Emma didn't hear the reply. It was as if she were in a tunnel and all she could see at the end of that dark void was Mark. His expression, his movements, his smile. He was the light in her life. Him and Angie.

The realization that she loved him left her shaking. She squeezed her eyes shut and took a deep, steadying breath.

"Emma? You okay?"

She focused on Mark's face. Holding a package of hot dogs, he stood before the counter, his concerned gaze resting on her. The noise from the crowd brought her back to reality.

"Yes, I'm fine." She picked up the tongs and placed a hot dog in the bun she held before putting it on a plate for the woman she had been serving.

Relief etched Mark's features. "Good. I was afraid you might be getting heat exhaustion."

"No, no, I'm fine."

An hour later, their replacements came to relieve them and Mark took Emma's arm as he led her deep into the park.

"I wonder where Angie is," he said, craning his neck to see through the crowd.

"No doubt having fun with her group."

They stopped at the dance platform where couples were doing the jitterbug. Over the speakers, Emma heard Little Richard singing "Tuttie Fruttie."

"Great song," Mark yelled above the deafening noise.

Emma hesitated, remembering her last anniversary with David, three months before Brian died. He'd held her close, his arms muscular and strong, but even then, she'd felt his aloofness and disapproval.

"Hey, Dad!"

Angie ran toward them, wearing a floppy Seven Dwarf's hat and sporting a red stain around her mouth from some Popsicle or punch.

"Come on, you guys. We're gonna miss the race." Angie tugged on Mark and Emma's arms.

Mark smiled at his daughter, thinking how good it

was to see her happy and animated. Laughing at her eagerness, he let her pull him and Emma over to the field where the three-legged race was about to start.

Standing at the entry line, Angie reached for a ball of twine and handed it to her dad. "I registered you for the race. Come on. Hurry!"

Mark saw Emma staring at the lineup where a multitude of parents and their children paired up with their inside legs bound together.

"You have got to be kidding. What have you gotten us into?" she asked Angie.

"Ah, come on, Emma," Mark urged. "It'll be fun."

The director of the race yelled through a megaphone that the race would start in five minutes. Kids and adults laughed, stretched and prepared for the race.

Mark thought of wrapping his arm around Emma and pulling her close as they ran toward the finish line. He couldn't wait.

Emma looked squeamish. Maybe he and Angie were pushing her too hard, too fast. But he hadn't had this much fun since—

He couldn't remember when. He'd never felt like this about any woman before, and he wasn't quite certain what it meant. He only knew he felt like laughing again. His heart swelled with joy and he didn't want it to end.

"Okay, but just this once." Emma warned as she took a deep breath.

"Hooray!" Angie jumped up and down, clapping her hands.

Sitting side by side in the grass, Mark tied his leg to Emma's. Angie took away the ball of twine while Mark and Emma wrapped their arms around each other's backs and stood, hobbling over to the starting line.

"You really think we can do this?" Emma asked, looking doubtful.

"Of course we can," he encouraged.

"But what if we lose?"

Mark tilted his head and studied her for a moment before he shrugged. "Who cares?"

She smiled up into his eyes and hugged him tighter. It felt so natural to be with her.

"All ready?" the coordinator of the race called through his megaphone.

A breathless pause filled the air.

"Oh, I hope you don't regret this," Emma whispered to Mark.

He chuckled. "Not one bit."

"On your mark … get set … Go!"

Mark took a step, trying not to lengthen his stride too wide for Emma to keep up. She held her own pretty well, matching his pace until the very end. The grassy field was bumpy and she stumbled in a hole. Down they went. Their arms and legs tangled, their laughter filled the air as they scrambled to regain their feet.

"Hurry, Dad! Hurry, Emma!" Angie screamed at them from the finish line.

Pulling Emma up, he settled her on her feet. She laughed so hard, she could hardly catch her breath. Tears ran from her eyes. Her long hair fell across her face and he couldn't resist sweeping it back from her cheeks.

"You okay?" he asked with concern. "You didn't twist your ankle, did you?"

"No, we're losing. Let's go!"

Off they went, hopping along until they collapsed once more over the finish line.

"Yea!" Angie fell on top of them. Her laughter mingled with theirs as she hugged and kissed them both.

"You guys were great! But you didn't win," she advised with a solemn expression.

"Did you really expect us to?" Emma giggled.

"Nah, but you still get a prize."

Angie pointed to a woman handing out consolation candy bars to all the participants.

Mark untied their legs and pulled Emma to her feet. Her eyes sparkled with happiness and her smile left him weak-kneed. He plucked blades of grass out of her hair and she stared into his eyes. Drawing near, he felt the sudden urge to kiss her.

She ducked her head and swiped at the grass and leaves on her clothes. The moment was broken and he stepped away.

"Well," he sighed. "It's about time for me to head over to the dunking booth."

Emma nodded. "Yeah, I guess so."

"Hey, Dad, can I jump on the trampoline?"

Looking down, he saw Angie pointing to a large trampoline set up beside the dunking booth. A man and little boy were holding hands as they bounced on it. Though it had tall netting guards circling it for safety, Mark shook his head. "I don't think that's a good idea, honey."

"Ah, but I want to. Please." Angie showed a dejected pout.

"If you stick that bottom lip out any further, you're gonna trip over it," he teased.

She scowled and Mark tossed a skeptical glance at Emma. "What do you think, Doc?"

"I don't see why not. Let her go, Mark."

"Pleeease, Dad." Angie jumped up and down, a hopeful expression on her pixie face.

It went against his better judgment, but how could he fight them both? Though Emma didn't say so, he knew he held Angie too tight. Surely it wouldn't hurt to let her go this time.

"All right," he laughed. "But only once."

Angie took off at a run toward the trampoline and Mark faced Emma. "Well, I'd better go. Duty calls."

"Yeah." There was a twinge of hesitancy in her voice.

"See you later?" he asked.

"Sure, you're my ride home," she reminded him.

A thrill of anticipation tingled over him, but Mark was loath to let her out of his sight. The only thing that sustained him was the knowledge that he'd get to see her later that evening.

Confident in this knowledge, he headed toward the dressing room, where he had left his towel and swim trunks.

As she walked across the park, Emma saw a sea of people surrounding the dunking booth. Drawing nearer, she stood on her tiptoes to peer over the heads of the crowd, trying to glimpse the glass walls of the water tank.

Mark sat inside on a bench hanging over the pool of clear water. He wore a pair of aqua-colored paisley swim trunks, revealing the lean, strong body he had earned from years of working out and staying active.

Wow, he looked great.

A crooked smile curved his mouth as he taunted the onlookers. "Come on, lay down your money. It's for a good cause. I dare you to knock me in."

Oh, it was too tempting. Emma couldn't resist.

"Excuse me." She elbowed her way through the crowd.

Reaching the booth operator, she handed the girl the tickets she had purchased earlier and picked up three yellow balls.

This was going to be fun!

Mark spied her and his brows lifted in surprise. He grinned and raised a long arm.

"Yeah, Emma. Woo-eee!" he called. "Go for it, girl. I dare you to knock me in."

She smiled with determination. In her mind, she couldn't prevent the words that filled her brain. *This is for dumping me for Denise Johnson.*

She pressed her tongue to the roof of her mouth and drew back her arm and fired. She hit the target dead-on and a loud bell rang. Down Mark went into the pool. He emerged soaking wet, flinging his head back to get the hair and water out of his eyes.

Satisfaction burned inside of Emma. She laughed and jumped up and down, filled with as much excitement as a schoolgirl.

"Burr!" Mark shivered as waves slapped him in the face. "This water is cold!"

His laughter joined with that of the crowd as they cheered for him to get back up on the plank.

"Good girl," Mark called to Emma as he climbed the ladder and sat on the platform. "I guess your throwing arm has improved since high school. See if you can do it again, babe."

Babe. The endearment went straight to her heart, burning there like a flame. Oh, yes, she could do it again. She would show him.

In her mind, more words filtered in and she didn't feel a bit of guilt as she lifted her arm. *This is for breaking my heart back when we were in high school.*

Again, she fired.

Ding!

Down he went into the water.

The crowd roared. Mark emerged, sputtering as he wiped his eyes and nose. His laughter rang out, low and masculine. What a good sport. Not only did she admire Mark, but she also respected him.

"I think you have a death wish for me," he crowed.

Now, her resentment seemed so childish. So shallow and unimportant. Her anger evaporated like summer mist across the Sierra Nevadas. Happiness bubbled up inside, her heart floating higher than the clouds.

"I've still got one more," she called as peals of laughter tumbled from her throat. "Get back on that seat, Williams, and let me have my money's worth."

A wide grin split his face and he jabbed a dripping finger toward her. "I'm gonna make you pay for this, Emma Shields. Just you wait until I'm out of this booth."

"I'm not afraid of you," she called as he climbed the ladder one more time.

Drawing back her arm, a third vendetta came to mind. *This is for making me fall in love with you!*

She threw the ball as hard as she could.

Ding!

Down he went.

The crowd went wild.

As Mark emerged once more from the pool, he sputtered and chuckled until his face flushed red.

The girl running the dunking booth presented Emma with a floppy brown teddy bear with a crooked black nose. Emma's sides hurt and tears squeezed from her eyes. No longer was she angry at anyone. Not at God, not at Mark, and not even at herself. The pain had been replaced with the insatiable desire to forgive. She had tried so hard to save Brian's life. But God had taken her little boy to be with Him. Knowing Brian was in the Lord's care brought her such solace. The more she loved, the more her capacity to love increased.

Was that what her prayers and the Atonement had done? It expelled her grief. It renewed her spirit. How grateful she was for her Savior's loving sacrifice for her.

Mark was My tool to bring you back to Me, child.

Uncertainty filled her. Once Angie's treatments were finished, they'd each move on. She wanted more, but what if Mark didn't have room in his life for her?

Chapter Seventeen

That evening Emma enjoyed quiet contentment as she sat in Mark's truck with Angie resting between them. Emma had given her bear to Angie, and the child promptly named it Teddy.

Holding the oversize bear close, Angie yawned and cuddled against Emma's side while her father drove Emma home. Emma wrapped her arm around Angie and eased the child's head against her chest so the girl would be more comfortable. Angie sighed, her rosebud mouth parted slightly as Emma relaxed her hand on the seat, close by Angie's leg. Feelings of unconditional love filled Emma to overflowing for this small girl and her father.

"She's really tired tonight," Emma observed.

Lighted lamps glowed overhead as they passed down the dark street. Mark glanced at his daughter, his hands on the steering wheel as he drove through traffic. "Yeah, she's had a busy day. You don't think she's overdone it, do you?"

Emma shook her head and smiled, brushing a crumb of ice-cream cone away from Angie's cheek. The girl's mouth was stained red from the cherry snowcone she had eaten earlier. "No, a little activity is good for her and her appetite today was voracious. I think I saw her put away an entire hamburger and hot dog, a candy apple and a cotton candy."

A sigh of disbelief escaped him. "I noticed that, too. It was good to see her so happy."

Mark's hand covered Emma's, startling her. Looking up, she met his intense gaze and his warm smile filled with unspoken promises. "I had a great time with you, Emma."

"Thanks. Me, too. But you better keep your eyes on the road," she teased.

He squeezed her hand as he focused on his driving. Their fingers entwined, as he drove her home in silence.

Parking in front of Emma's duplex, Mark hopped out and came to help her down from the truck. Angie didn't move a muscle as Emma laid her on the seat, then withdrew slowly. Oh, how Emma wished she could stay. It felt comfortable and natural to be with them. It felt odd to leave.

Mark clasped Emma's hand in his as he walked with her up the sidewalk. The dark sky showed bright twinkling stars and a round moon to guide their way. The chirp of crickets filled the air along with the sweet aroma of Emma's honeysuckle bush.

At her doorstep Mark took hold of both Emma's hands and faced her. She stared up into his eyes, mesmerized by the depth of emotion she saw there. His eyes seemed to mirror what she was feeling inside.

"Thank you for a wonderful day," she said.

"It was wonderful because of you," he whispered.

"I think Angie had fun, too."

He stepped nearer and her heart began to hammer. "Yes, she had a blast. Thanks again for the teddy bear. It means a lot to her, even if you did dunk me three times to win it."

Emma gave a throaty laugh. "It was my pleasure."

He grinned. "I'd take a dunking from you anytime, lady."

Their smiles faded slowly. His head lowered until he kissed her ever so gently on the lips. He tasted of spearmint and smelled of grass and barbecue. When his arms folded around her and he pulled her close, she hugged him back. It felt so right being in his arms and she longed to stay like this forever.

"I want to see you again, Emma," he whispered against her lips. "I'm tired of pretending I don't care about you. I want us to be much more than just friends."

Her heart did myriad flipflops. "I'd like that, too, Mark. I never thought I'd feel this way again. I love being with you and Angie."

His eyes darkened, his nose touching hers. She inched closer and he kissed her one more time.

"Are you available tomorrow around one o'clock?" he asked.

As she nodded, she tried to calm her erratic breathing.

"Good. Come on over to my house. You haven't eaten until you've tried some of my homemade potato salad and barbecued chicken."

A thrill of expectancy caused her pulse to skitter. "I'd like that very much. I'll bring dessert."

"Chocolate-chip cookies?" He winked at her.

She tilted her head back and laughed. "We'll see. Maybe I can make something different this time."

His sigh of pleasure warmed her cheek. "I'm sure it'll be delicious."

As he withdrew, his fingers slid down her forearm to her hand, caressing her palm until only their fingertips touched. Warmth tingled up her arm, his touch electric. A lock of sand-colored hair fell over his brow.

"See you tomorrow," she said, liking the way his eyes twinkled when he smiled.

He ambled toward his truck and Emma bit her tongue to keep from calling him back. She longed for him to stay, to talk and laugh some more. She didn't want it to end. But they had tomorrow to look forward to, and the future opened up from there.

As she stood on her doorstep she wrapped her arms around her waist and watched him get into the truck. When he pulled away and rounded the corner, he waved before he disappeared from view.

Begrudgingly, Emma went inside her duplex. Tomorrow. He would call her and they would spend time together and talk and laugh with Angie and—

She would never be lonely again.

Elation swept her. She hadn't realized how lost she'd been these past two years. Not until Mark had made her see how her anger had eaten up all her joy. Never had she looked forward to the rising of the sun with such anticipation. It would be hard to sleep tonight.

Walking into her bedroom, she flipped on the light and pulled the covers back on her bed. As she took a nightgown from the top drawer of her dresser, she caught sight of Brian's picture and paused, picking it up. Though she thought of her son every day, it had been several weeks since she had talked to his picture. Her thoughts had been filled with Mark and Angie, not the past.

She sat on the bed and stared at the picture of Brian wearing his favorite baseball cap. His wide smile showed a front tooth missing, and she remembered the day she had taken this picture just after they had returned from a family picnic at the lake.

"I haven't meant to ignore you, swcctheart," she said to him. "It's just that, well, would you mind terribly if I got on with my life?"

Reaching forward, she caressed the glass with her fingertips. "Since you left me, I've been so dead inside. Then Mark and Angie came into my office and I've discovered I want to live again."

Tears tumbled down her face and she dashed them away.

"You'll always be a part of me."

The wedge of guilt that had been lodged in her heart for so long was no longer there. It had simply lifted, freeing her of a burden that had become heavy and choking. Was it her imagination that Brian's smile deepened?

Bending her head, she kissed the glass pane, then set the picture on her nightstand. Somehow, looking at him brought her joy and confidence instead of wrenching pain.

Peace enveloped her as she slid between the cool sheets. Her gaze lingered on Brian's picture and her eyelids grew heavy.

Tomorrow. She would go to Mark's home and begin a new life with him and Angie. No longer did she dread the future. God had worked a miracle in her life and she felt embraced by His unparalleled love.

Chapter Eighteen

Mark parked his truck in the driveway and got out. The cool night air embraced him as he walked around to the passenger side to open the door and reach in for Angie. She still slept and he slid her into his arms, cradling her as he carried her up the walkway to his front door. The streetlight buzzed overhead and a chilly breeze swept past him.

Summer was almost over. Except for Angie's illness, it had been idyllic, sharing happy memories with Emma. At times, he could almost forget Angie's tumor and his divorce. He would never forget this day as long as he lived.

As he brushed past the row of trimmed box elders skirting the sidewalk, he stepped up on the front porch and noticed the living room light was on. Had he or Angie forgotten to turn it off?

He frowned and juggled Angie in his arms as he reached into his pants' pocket for his house key. Inserting it into the lock, he was about to turn the knob when the door opened and light flooded him from the entranceway.

"Denise!"

He stared at his ex-wife as she stood before him wearing a bright pink tank top with spaghetti straps and a short denim skirt. Her stiletto heels showed off her long, slender legs, though he wondered how she could walk without strutting like a peacock. Her bleached-blond hair hung past her shoulders in long, thin strands and her eyeliner made her eyes appear heavy and shadowed.

"Thank goodness you're finally home." She practically gushed, reaching to pull him inside. "Where have you been all day? I've been waiting for hours."

When he realized his mouth hung open, he closed it and stepped into the formal living room with Angie still sleeping in his arms. "How did you get in here?"

She reached for the cherrywood table sitting beneath a gilded mirror in the main foyer and dangled a key in front of his nose. "I used my house key, silly."

He sucked back an irritated sigh, making a mental note to change all the locks in the house as soon as possible. He had planned to do it a while ago, but hadn't found the time. He'd make it a priority tomorrow morning, before Emma arrived.

"I still don't understand why you're here so late." He shouldered past, carrying Angie toward the stairs.

Her heels tapped behind him as she followed him across the entranceway. At the bottom of the stairs, he pivoted to look at her. His arms started to ache under Angie's weight. "I'll take Angie up to bed and then we can talk."

He turned toward the stairs and caught sight of her two large suitcases sitting beside the wall. He angled his head to look at Denise again and jerked his chin toward the bags. "What's this?"

"My things." She shrugged her slim shoulders and opened her arms wide. "You're always asking me to come and visit Angie. Well, here I am."

What was going on? He knew his ex-wife too well. Something was up. He could see it in the way she wrung her hands together and chewed her bottom lip. She wanted something. After the tidy settlement he'd given her in their divorce, he wondered what more she could want.

"Denise, you can't stay here—"

"Mommy?" Angie woke up and rubbed her eyes. "Mommy!"

She squirmed in his arms and Mark placed her on her feet, wishing she had slept long enough for him to get her to bed. He didn't want her to witness an argument between him and Denise.

Angie tottered on her feet and he reached to steady her.

"Mommy!" She raced toward her mother, throwing her frail arms around Denise's waist.

"Oh, Angie!" Denise cried as she went down on one knee and hugged the girl. She didn't kiss her daughter. Mark knew Denise hated smudging her lipstick.

Angie squeezed Denise around the neck. As she held her child, Denise pulled her head back, so Angie wouldn't muss her hair.

"Hi, Angie. Oh, I've missed you so much." Denise pulled her daughter close to her chest.

Confusion filled Mark's mind. He couldn't remember the last time Denise had been this affectionate with their daughter. Maybe the long absence had caused her to appreciate Angie more.

"Why haven't you called me?" Angie asked, her words muffled against her mother's arm.

"Well, I tried. But every time I called, I got a busy signal or your Dad told me you were off playing somewhere."

"You didn't leave us any messages," Angie pointed out.

"Oh, well, I didn't want to talk to the machine. I wanted to talk to you in person."

Mark bit the inside of his mouth to keep from saying something derogatory in front of his daughter. He didn't want to hurt Angie, but he planned to have a strong talk with Denise later on, in private.

"Where's your Jaguar?" he asked. "I didn't see it parked outside."

"I sold it." Denise stood and waved a hand in the air as she stepped away from Angie.

Without her mother's support, Angie swayed on her feet. She needed sleep.

"Hey, honey, let's get you upstairs." Mark reached for her.

"Can't I stay with Mommy?" Angie clasped her mother's hand.

Foreboding settled over Mark as Denise breezed into the family room with Angie, their arms locked together. A lump formed in Mark's throat when he saw how fiercely Angie held on to her mother.

"Are you home for good?" Angie asked.

"Well, that depends on your dad." Denise tossed a hopeful look at Mark.

"Daddy doesn't mind," Angie said. "He wants you here, don't you, Dad?"

Angie wore an innocent smile and Mark couldn't bear to break her heart. No, he didn't want Denise here.

She was not staying. They were no longer married and his thoughts lingered on Emma.

He decided to let Angie spend a few minutes more with her mom. Then, he'd put his daughter to bed, call Denise a cab and face the fallout with Angie the next morning when she asked where her mother had gone.

They ignored him as they snuggled together on the couch. Shaking his head, Mark sat in a chair by the big-screen TV. Denise spoke to Angie in muted tones. The child just listened, rubbing her eyes, her movements sluggish. Though being with her mother elated Angie, this wasn't a good time for a visit.

"Honey, do you feel okay?" he asked.

Angie nodded, her eyelids drooping.

"Why don't you go upstairs and get into bed, now?" Denise suggested. "Then, Daddy and I can have a long talk and we can do something fun together in the morning."

"Okay, but Emma's coming over." Angie smothered a yawn as she slid off the couch and stood before her mother.

Mark tensed. His plans for tomorrow didn't include Denise.

"Emma?" Denise glanced at Mark. "Emma who?"

"She's my doctor." Angie spoke in a vague tone as she stifled another yawn.

Denise's eyes narrowed and her mouth hardened. "Oh. Anyone I know?"

"It's Emma Clemmons," Mark explained. "Her name's Shields, now. She's Angie's oncologist."

"Oh, *her.*" Denise gave a piercing laugh. "A married woman, Mark?"

He tightened his hands. "She's divorced, just like me."

Her mouth rounded. "So, she became a doctor, hmm?"

"Yeah, and she's pretty," Angie said.

"Yes, she is," Mark agreed.

Denise's mouth hardened. "But why would you invite her here, Mark? I mean, she's got to be the most boring person I know."

Mark clenched his jaw. Boring? He'd never met a more exciting woman. Bright, intelligent, giving, and too dignified to ever pout or pretend tears. Real. Emma didn't play games to get what she wanted.

He sat forward, prepared to defend Emma, but Angie cut him off. "Emma makes us cookies, and her and Dad almost won the three-legged race."

"Oh, really? She sounds very…domestic." There was a hard edge to Denise's tone.

"This will be fun." Angie showed a slight smile. "We can have a party and you can meet Emma. I'm so glad you're home, Mommy. Don't ever leave us again, okay?"

Angie wrapped her spindly arms around her mother's neck and hugged tight. A hard lump settled in Mark's stomach.

"Of course I'll stay." Denise's gaze lifted to Mark's and she stared at him from over the top of Angie's head.

Mark didn't smile or speak a word. He didn't want to encourage Denise or upset Angie. This was happening too fast. He needed time to think. To sort this out. Denise was *not* staying, that was a given. But he felt torn when Angie smiled at him. He wanted to reach an agreement with Denise for regular visitations at a reasonable time of day, but he feared he might say something to drive her away from Angie. No matter what, he couldn't allow Denise to hold him hostage with their daughter.

He returned Angie's smile and stood up before he squeezed her arm. "Why don't you run upstairs and get ready for bed? You and I will talk about this later."

Seeming confident to have her parents back together, Angie turned and stumbled.

"Whoa, careful there, sweetheart."

Angie put a hand to her head, blinking her eyes.

"Are you dizzy?" Mark scooped her into his arms and tossed a look in Denise's direction. "I'll take her up and be right back."

He left Denise, grateful for the distraction as he walked with his cherished burden to her bedroom. Sitting her on the bed, he opened Angie's dresser drawer, wishing again that his ex-wife hadn't showed up like this unannounced.

"Time to sleep," he urged.

Angie curled up on her covers, closing her eyes. "But I want to see Mommy."

He sighed and rested one hand on the top dresser drawer. "I know you do, hon."

A deep huff of air trembled from her chest as her eyelids dipped low. He decided it would be okay to let her stay in her shorts and he removed her shoes, then covered her with a blanket. They'd brush her teeth extra well in the morning.

He walked back downstairs, his thoughts a jumbled mass of confusion. He searched his heart, finding no romantic love for his ex-wife. Except for Angie's sake, Mark had no desire to see Denise again.

In sharp contrast, he couldn't wait to see Emma. He wanted to plan a future with her. In all their years of courtship and marriage, he had never felt as happy around Denise as he did with Emma. Not even in high school. Ah, he had been so foolish to ever give Emma up.

Breathing deeply, he made his way downstairs, bracing himself for whatever might follow. As he walked into the kitchen, he heard his ex-wife on the phone, talking to her mother.

"No, Mom. I'll stay here tonight. I can put up with him and the kid, as long as he pays the bills."

So, that was it. Denise was broke. How had she gone through all that money so soon?

Mark clenched his hands. Every nerve in his body felt like exploding.

Muttering under his breath, he opened the fridge. He made no pretense of being quiet as he took out a dozen eggs, then slammed the door closed. He placed the eggs in a pan to boil and flipped on the burner. He didn't want to eavesdrop on his ex-wife.

"Oh, he's back." Denise's harsh whisper came from the living room. "I've got to go."

He hardened his jaw as he opened the pantry to take out a bucket of russet potatoes. He'd get them cooked and in the refrigerator tonight so they would chill for his potato salad tomorrow morning.

Emma. The thought of seeing her again eased his mind and gave him the focus he needed.

Denise glided into the room, glancing at the boiling eggs. She sat on one of the tall bar stools at the counter, acting like she owned the place. He could feel her gaze drilling into him as he turned the heat down on the stove. The low clacking of the boiling eggs filled the void.

She inhaled a deep breath, then crinkled her nose. "What is that awful smell?"

He didn't look at her as he sorted the mail. "Boiled eggs. I'm making potato salad."

"It stinks up the whole house." She grimaced.

Setting the mail aside, he placed his hands on the counter and looked straight at her. "What are you doing here, Denise?"

She leaned forward on the bar, exposing her ample cleavage to his view. He knew her moves so well, he didn't even glance down. "I told you, I came to see Angie."

He looked away and breathed deep, pulling air into his lungs like it might clear his tension. "I'm glad, for Angie's sake, but I would rather you called first. I don't want you coming into my home again without being invited."

Rounding the counter, he picked up a stack of financial statements he planned to review for a client before he went to bed.

She patted the stool next to her. "I need to talk with you about some things. Come and sit by me."

He moved to the stove and made a pretense of checking the eggs. "If you sold the Jag, how did you get here? I didn't see another car out front."

"Oh, um, I took a cab. I don't have a car right now."

"No car? What did you do with the money you got for the Jaguar?"

She lifted a hand and waved it in the air. "I had expenses. It's not your business anyway."

He quirked a brow at her. "It's my business if you've come to ask me for more money."

Her mouth dropped open as he stood at the sink, scrubbing the potatoes. He pricked them with a fork, then popped them into the microwave to cook. "I'll call you a cab to take you to your mother's or a motel, whichever you prefer."

He reached for the cordless phone.

"Wait!"

He paused and she ducked her head, her eyes filled with remorse. "I want to apologize, Mark. I realize how unfair I've been to you and Angie. I never meant to hurt you. Say you'll forgive me. Say you'll let me come back home. You're a Christian and Christians forgive, right?"

He snorted. "Forgive, yes, but God doesn't want me to trash my life. Why the sudden change of heart?"

He wanted to hear it from her own lips. She wasn't motivated by love.

As she placed her hands on his chest and pressed closer, Mark caught the scent of her perfume. The heavy aroma no longer attracted him like Emma's clean smell and he held his breath.

"I made a mistake and I want to come home."

He walked into the family room, picking up Angie's books and toys and tidying the house. He wasn't certain how to pull it off without a fight, but he wanted Denise to leave. Right now.

Denise trailed after him like a puppy on a leash.

"All right! Eric left me," she whined.

Mark sighed. "Did he leave you for a younger woman or because you're broke?"

Her face whitened. "Both. I made some bad investments and the money's all gone. He found someone new."

Well, well. Chickens were roosting tonight.

Although she deserved it, he pitied his ex-wife and didn't want to hurt her. In fact, he didn't feel anything for her now. Loving Emma had taken the sting of the divorce away. Yet, he hated the thought that Denise would use him to get more.

"I suggest you stay with your mother until you can find yourself a job. If you want to see Angie, we can arrange that at a more reasonable time of day."

"A job?"

"Yeah." He nodded. "You might find it fun and fulfilling to work."

"But I've never worked before. What can I do?" Her eyes widened, as if she had something stuck on the bottom of her expensive shoes.

"Maybe you could go to beauty school and learn to be a hairdresser," he suggested. "You've always liked the salons."

"I like fixing my own hair, not other people's."

"Daddy?"

Angie came into the room wearing her slippers and the shorts he had put her to bed in. She stood in the doorway, blinking her eyes as if she could hardly keep them open.

"Daddy, I don't feel good. Can I have a drink of water?"

"Oh, Angie," Denise huffed, and waved the child off. "Can't you see your Dad and I are having an important conversation?"

"Sure, honey, let me get you a drink." Mark smiled to cover Denise's rebuke and went to the kitchen for a cup. Denise followed, shifting her weight on the granite floor of the dining room.

Cold and hard as her heart.

Mark took the cup back to Angie, with Denise hot on his heels. Angie slumped against the wall.

"Are you okay, honey?" he asked.

Denise snorted. "Angie, go back to bed now."

"Don't speak to my daughter that way," Mark snapped.

He picked Angie up, cradling her against his chest. She closed her eyes. He'd never seen her so tired before.

Mark carried her to her room and put her back in bed. He used the upstairs phone to call a cab. Twenty minutes later he carried Denise's suitcases outside. She had no option but to follow. He held the door for her while she slid inside the car, her back stiff with anger. Without a word, he closed the car door, then gave the cabdriver the address to her mother's house and a twenty-dollar bill.

As the car pulled away from the curb and turned the corner, he couldn't help think about Angie crying for her mother. Her tears haunted him and niggling doubt ate at the corners of his mind.

What if becoming Angie's stepmom proved too much for Emma? She'd already lost her own son. What if he married her and she abandoned them, just like Denise? It would be too much. He and Angie couldn't stand another heartache like that.

Neither could Emma.

Chapter Nineteen

At precisely eleven o'clock the next morning, Emma lifted a homemade deep-dish apple pie from her oven and set it to cool on the countertop. She smiled at the bubbly juice and golden crust baked to perfection. Mark and Angie were going to love it with vanilla ice cream.

Her phone rang and she wiped her hands on a dish towel before answering the call.

"Hello?"

A long pause followed.

"Um, hi, Emma." Mark's voice sounded tired and strained.

"Well, hi, stranger. I hope you've got the barbecue fired up, because I've got a fierce appetite for chicken today."

"Uh, yeah, that's why I'm calling, Emma. I'm sorry, but I'm going to have to cancel. Something unavoidable came up."

Knots of disappointment tightened in Emma's stomach. "Nothing serious, I hope."

His deep sigh rasped through the receiver. "Nothing

for you to worry about. Just a personal matter I need to deal with."

"I understand. What about dinner tomorrow night?"

Another long pause. "No, I can't. I'm…I'm buried with work. I'm sorry, but I think it'd be best if we don't see each other for a while."

His words crushed her heart. She licked her lips as the ramifications spilled over her in crashing waves. "Mark, I don't understand. What's going on?"

"Nothing for you to worry about. I'm sorry, Emma. It's just that…I think with Angie's illness and everything going on at work, it would be best for all of us if I don't complicate matters with a new relationship right now."

Emma held her breath. Beads of perspiration broke out on her forehead and the back of her neck. He was breaking up with her and she didn't know why. "That's it? You don't want to *complicate* your life with me?"

She tried to stop it, but her voice sounded harsh with frustration and hurt. Her heart pounded in her ears. She could hardly believe he would do this without a more logical explanation. And over the phone, no less.

"No, it's not like that, Emma. You've been great. It's just that—I don't want to hurt you any more. I think you've been through enough."

"Hurt me? Like you're hurting me now?"

The silence on the phone sounded deafening.

"Look, Mark, if you're getting cold feet, we can slow things down. I never meant to be pushy."

"No, you haven't pushed me to do anything I didn't want to. I just need to concentrate on Angie right now. I can't explain it better than that. Please, try to understand."

She blinked hot tears from her eyes. "But I thought we were working to get Angie better."

He didn't respond right away. When he did, she heard the tension in his voice. He sounded agitated and harried. "I'm sorry, Emma. Look, I've got to go. You take care of yourself, okay?"

Like he really cared.

"Yeah, thanks for the call, Mark. Give Angie my love." Bitterness laced every word.

"I will. I'm sorry, Emma. Goodbye."

He hung up. She stood frozen, pressing the receiver against her cheek until the dial tone buzzed in her ear.

She finally hung up the phone. She turned and stumbled before she gripped the back of a chair to steady herself. Her gaze swept the room, seeing everything as if she were in a tunnel. Torn with confusion, she tried to comprehend what had just happened. Why would Mark break up with her so suddenly over the phone? It didn't make sense.

She stared at the warm pie. Without thinking, she picked it up and carried it to the garbage can, her steps stiff with anger. She lifted the lid and dropped it inside where it landed with a loud thump. As she dusted off her hands, she ignored the tears streaming down her face.

For the second time in her life, Emma had lost the man she loved. She felt just like that abandoned pie. Its fluted edges carefully molded and teased before being discarded in the trash and forgotten.

It wouldn't happen a third time. She had learned her lesson. She was an educated woman, strong and independent. Mark Williams would never use her again.

* * *

Mark didn't call. Emma stayed by the phone all day, hoping this was a terrible mistake and he would tell her he didn't mean it and set things straight. Something had caused him to break up with her, but she couldn't think what it might be.

She thought about going over to his house, to demand a better explanation, but decided against it. He needed time to sort it out. Pressuring him wouldn't help.

By early evening Emma picked up the telephone receiver, aching to hear his voice again.

She dropped the receiver into its cradle. Mark would have to call her. She deserved that much respect. He had to make the next move. But deep inside, she knew something was terribly wrong.

Emma tidied her kitchen to keep busy. It didn't help much. She missed Mark's deep laughter and Angie's sweet hugs. It was her own fault she had allowed them to get under her skin, giving them the power to hurt her. She had known better than to open her heart. And yet, if she hadn't done so, she might never have recognized how wrong she was to abandon God.

What a fool to let Mark kiss her. To believe she meant anything to him.

She dashed angry tears from her cheeks, then jerked a tissue from the box sitting next to the couch and blew her nose.

Be calm. All is well.

The words echoed in her heart and left her confused, yet she knew it did no good fretting over something out of her control.

The phone rang and Emma jumped. Expectation

thrummed through her body. Sitting up on the sofa, she swallowed, not daring to hope it was Mark. Her hand shook as she picked up the receiver.

"Hello?"

"Hi, Emma. It's Sonja. How are you tonight?"

Disappointment lodged in Emma's throat. "I'm fine, Sonja. What's up?"

"Well, I was at the hospital visiting an old friend and I saw Mark Williams there."

Emma's spine stiffened. "What? Mark was at the hospital?"

"Yes. They rushed Angie into emergency surgery this afternoon. Apparently she hemorrhaged on the entire right side of her head."

"What?" Emma covered her face with one hand. "Is she all right?"

Sonja's sigh filtered through the receiver. "I think so, but Mark looked pretty shaken up. Angie had just gotten out of surgery when I saw him. He hadn't been allowed to see her yet, so I don't know what the prognosis is."

"Did he say what caused the hemorrhage?" Emma's voice sounded unusually shrill and she gripped the phone to steady herself.

"No, he didn't say. He seemed distracted and in a big hurry to see Angie, so I didn't detain him. I know you've become quite attached to them, so I thought I'd let you know."

Attached? That was putting it mildly. Emma loved them dearly. If anything happened to Angie—

Her chest tightened. She wanted to wail and scream. This wasn't fair. Not now. Not after everything else Angie had been through.

Why hadn't Mark told her?

"Thanks for calling to tell me, Sonja. I've got to get down there to check on them."

"Okay, Emma. I won't keep you any longer. Would you call me later tonight to let me know how Angie's doing? I think our entire office is worried about that little girl. We've all become attached to her."

"Yeah, sure. I'll call later." Emma spoke absentmindedly, her thoughts consumed with getting to the hospital. A hemorrhage of this type was highly unusual.

She hung up the phone, then dashed for her purse and car keys. What a dope she had been to believe Mark's pathetic explanation about why they shouldn't see each other anymore. Angie had gone into emergency surgery and Mark hadn't told her. That was a hard slap in the face, yet Emma understood his reticence. She had to get to Mark, to look him in the eye and tell him—

She froze.

Tell him what? That she could go through this again with him and Angie? That she didn't mind pacing the floor of the hospital and wringing her hands with anguish, her heart tearing to shreds when she got the fatal news?

Her entire body trembled. It would be more than difficult for her to go into the pediatric ward of the hospital. She hadn't been there since the night Brian—

She didn't want to go. She wanted to stay home, where she wouldn't feel bereft and helpless. It was safe here. No worry, no fears.

No love.

Maybe Mark had been right not to tell her the truth, after all. She couldn't go. She just couldn't.

Chapter Twenty

Mark eased his head back against the lumpy recliner and closed his weary eyes. A clipboard and several insurance forms lay sprawled across his lap. More paperwork. At this point, he ought to have a Masters degree in medical procedures.

He blew out a breath. As he rested his hands on top of the papers, they made a crackling noise. The intensive care unit looked dark, except for a single lamp resting on a table beside Angie's bed. The smell of antiseptic and ammonia permeated the air and he wrinkled his nose.

What time was it?

Opening his eyes, he peered through the dark at his wristwatch. Almost eleven o'clock. Where had this day gone?

He squinted at the fine print on the documents and tried to scratch out another response on the form. It was no use. He was exhausted, emotionally and physically. He longed to call Emma, to ask her to come be with him, but he couldn't bring himself to do it. She'd been through so much pain. She had shared her deepest feelings about her son's death and he couldn't ask her to go through that again with him and Angie. It had broken his heart to call and tell Emma he didn't want to see her anymore, but he made the sacrifice thinking it best for her.

He tossed the pen aside and glanced about the expansive room Angie shared with four other patients. Each of the beds had a white sliding curtain pulled between them, to offer a bit of privacy. The curtains hung like ghoulish ghosts hovering in the dark.

Yesterday, the Make-A-Wish barbecue had been wonderful. Then, he had kissed Emma good-night and confided that he wanted to be more than friends. He meant it, but now—

Angie lay sleeping beside him, flat on her back, hooked up to four IVs and a brain drain. Her bald head was stained with orange antiseptic and stitches.

Oh, baby, look what they've done to you this time.

He'd been a fool to think he could involve Emma in this. Reaching out, he stroked Angie's arm, his fingers evading the tangle of tubes.

"Don't worry, bug." He spoke in a trembling whisper. "We can recover from this. Your hair will grow back. It's going to be okay."

Though Angie slept, he needed to hear the words. To give himself strength. He hadn't been able to speak with the neurosurgeon since he'd come out of the operating room to say Angie was stable. But what about tomorrow, and the next day after that?

Please, Father, please don't take her from me. I've already lost Emma. I can't lose them both.

Angie's eyes fluttered open and she blinked. "Daddy?"

Her voice sounded hoarse from the tubes they'd put down her throat and he leaned near. He cupped her cheek with his hand as he placed a careful kiss on her nose. He tried to smile, but his lips trembled and he feared he might break down and cry. It was important that he remain strong for her. "Hi, honey-girl. How are you doing?"

"Okay." She tried to sit up. "Is Mommy here?"

"Lay still, babe." He pressed a hand to her chest. "Remember, you need to lie flat until the brain drain runs clear. Then, the nurse will take out the IVs and let you up and we can get you something to eat."

"Okay." She lay perfectly still, knowing this routine so well. "Where's Mommy?"

He had no idea. He had tried to call Denise at her mother's house and left several messages, but she hadn't returned his calls. Not that he expected her to. "Mommy couldn't make it. How do you feel? Are you in any pain?"

"No, I want Emma. Is she here?" Angie's voice quavered and a tear ran from her eye and down the side of her face.

He wiped it away. "No, honey, but I am."

Oh, how he missed Emma.

"You're always here, Dad."

"Are you hungry?" Mark tried to distract her.

The girl took a deep breath and let it go. "No, just tired."

He bit the inside of his mouth. Being hungry was a good sign and he wished she would ask for a rack of beef ribs to eat. "Then, sleep. In the morning, we can talk. You're doing just fine, sweetheart. Everything's going to be okay."

She licked her dry lips and gave a vague nod. Her fingers curled around his thumb, her hand frail.

"Are you cold, honey?"

She gave a subtle shake of her head.

"Well, your skin feels chilled. Let's cover you, just in case." He spread another blanket over her and smoothed it across her spindly legs.

"Daddy?"

"Hmm?"

"Am I gonna die?"

He froze, staring at her face. His heart shredded as tears burned his eyes. She had asked this of Emma weeks ago, when Mrs. Valdez passed away. Here it was again. The uncertainty. The fear.

Careful of her IVs and keeping her flat on her back, he pressed his arms around her and kissed her face and neck repeatedly. "No, honey. I won't let you."

A sob rose in his throat but he pushed it down. He couldn't let her see him weep. He must give her hope.

Perhaps it was futile to promise such a thing, but he couldn't bear to tell his precious child the truth…that she could die. They all would someday. Only God knew when. But for his child—any child—to die this way was incredibly unfair.

He felt helpless. Lost. Without his faith in God, he couldn't be strong. How had Emma managed to survive the death of her child without God by her side?

The answer was simple. She hadn't. Not at all.

"Mrs. Miller says I'm heaven sent." Angie's soft voice made him draw back to look at her eyes.

He kept one hand against her face, so she could feel him and take comfort in his presence.

He cleared his throat. "Mrs. Miller, the candy striper?"

"Yes, she's my new friend."

Angie had a way of making friends everywhere she went. Even now, stuffed animals and flowers surrounded her room and he didn't know half the people here at the hospital who had given them to her.

"Well, Mrs. Miller is right." He hunched one shoulder against his face to wipe his tears away.

"But to be heaven sent, don't I have to be dead?"

Mark gave a shaky laugh. "No, honey. You're very much alive. You're the most wonderful person I know."

"But I don't do anything, Dad. Not like you."

He gave a shuddering laugh. "If you only knew how much joy you bring me. Our Heavenly Father sends people into our lives to give us strength when our troubles become too burdensome to carry on our own."

"What people?"

"Well, people like Mrs. Miller."

Her forehead crinkled. "And Emma?"

His throat tightened and tears ran freely down his face. He couldn't stop their flow to save his life. "Especially Emma."

Angie's chest lifted in a deep sigh and she closed her eyes. "I think you and Emma are my special guardians."

Mark blinked, not surprised by her grown-up vocabulary. It was true. He remembered how worldly he had been before Angie's birth, caring about nothing but possessions and advancement in his profession. Then, when he had held his newborn daughter in his arms, he had realized wealth and prestige meant nothing without someone to love.

Her breathing evened out as she drifted back to sleep

and he pulled the blankets higher about her throat. "Go to sleep, little sweetheart. Everything will be better in the morning."

Sitting back in his chair, his gaze remained glued on Angie's face, watching her sleep, reticent to look away for even a moment.

As he reached for his paperwork, a movement caught his eye and he pivoted toward the doorway.

"Emma!"

She stood in the shadowed threshold, leaning the side of her head against the doorjamb, her eyes deep pools of misery as she stared at him.

Had she heard his conversation with Angie?

She took a deep breath and stepped into the darkened room, as if she were diving into a pool of great white sharks. Mark stood and walked to her, speaking in hushed tones so he wouldn't disturb Angie and the other sleeping children. "What are you doing here?"

"I just heard about Angie and came as fast as I could. I wanted to see that she was all right." Emma sounded rather breathless, as though she had run up a flight of stairs. She glanced around the room, her eyes wide with panic.

"You shouldn't be here, Emma."

"I had to come."

Her eyes met his, filled with such anguish it nearly broke his heart. He knew how hard it was for her to come to the pediatric ward, yet she made this sacrifice for him and Angie.

How happy he was to see her. The urge to take her into his arms filled him. He longed to hold her against his chest, to confide all his fears. Instead he slipped his hands into his pants' pockets. "How did you know we were here?"

"Sonja called me at home. Mark, why didn't you tell me?"

Heat flushed his face. "You've been through enough with your son and there was nothing you could do here."

"I could be here for you."

What could he say to that? He wanted her here with him, but he also longed to protect her. Keeping her in the dark about Angie was the only way he knew to do that. His good intentions had failed.

A flicker of doubt flashed in her eyes and her gaze slid over Angie. "How's she doing?"

He shrugged and glanced at his daughter. "As well as can be expected."

"Do you know what caused the hemorrhage?"

He hardened his jaw. "Yes, the neurosurgeon believes the combination of chemo drugs and the VP shunt caused it. When Angie jumped on the trampoline, there wasn't enough cushion in her head and it caused blood vessels to rupture."

A low moan escaped Emma's lips. "Oh, Mark, I'm so sorry. If I had known this might happen, I would never have encouraged you to let her jump. It's my fault—"

"It's *not* your fault." He cut her off. "No one could have anticipated this outcome. It just happened."

"But I told you it was okay. What must you think of me?"

I love you. That's what I think of you. He almost blurted the words to her, but bit the inside of his mouth instead.

He didn't blame Emma for what had happened. The

neurosurgeon had told him this was a fluke, something no one could have foreseen.

Emma's gaze locked with his. "Angie's right. You are her guardian, Mark. She's so lucky to have a father like you."

So, she had overheard his conversation with Angie. "I thought you didn't believe in God; that you only believe in science."

"Not anymore. I was so foolish, Mark. When my son died, I was angry and hurt. Blaming God, made my own pain easier to bear. I know now how wrong I was. I believe everything you've told me. I believe in you."

He snorted. "I can't save your soul, Emma. Only God can do that."

"You're right. With God in my life, I don't feel alone anymore. You gave me that sweet gift, Mark."

"It wasn't your fault Brian died, you know."

She looked away, her eyes swimming with tears. "Yes, it was."

A frown furrowed his forehead. "Why do you blame yourself?"

Her voice trembled and she wouldn't meet his eyes. "I was a new oncologist and thought I knew everything. I convinced Brian's doctors to try a new, radical chemo protocol. I truly believed it would save Brian's life, but it didn't work and he died. If I hadn't interfered, Brian might still be alive today. And now—" Her voice cracked. "Now, I gave you bad advice and Angie could die because of it."

Emma wrapped her arms around herself, looking so alone, so lost, her eyes red, her chin quivering. He took a step toward her, his arms lifting to enfold her against his chest. He caught himself just in time, before he told her how much he loved her. He longed to comfort her, but that would entail more commitment. She was already upset. How could he ask her to stay and watch Angie suffer as Brian had?

He couldn't.

"Don't, Emma. You did what you thought was best. Maybe a different chemo protocol would have given the same results." He paused, studying her wretched expression. How he hated to see her hurting like this.

Because he loved her, he must send her away.

"Look, Emma, it's hard to accept God's will, but I have to face the reality that I could lose Angie."

"I wish you had called me when she went into surgery. You needn't have suffered alone, Mark. Surely when we're hurting, our Heavenly Father weeps with us. I wanted to be here for you, to help you through it."

Rolling his shoulders, he stepped over to the chair, putting distance between them. "I'm used to handling things on my own."

She lifted a hand and tried to reach for him, but he backed away. His body language was stiff and unyielding, his expression closed. They were silent then, as though they had nothing left to say. So many words swirled around inside Emma's mind, yet she didn't dare speak what was in her heart.

Together, they stared at Angie and time spun away.

A buzzer went off on the other side of the room and a nurse came in to check on another patient.

Emma stepped nearer to Mark, hungry for the familiarity they had shared the day before. Somehow, that closeness was gone now and they seemed like strangers. "Is there anything I can do?"

"No, thank you."

Her throat felt like sandpaper. She clenched her hands until she felt the bite of her fingernails digging into her palms.

He raked a hand through his tussled hair. Fatigue creased his forehead and eyes. He looked careworn and Emma longed to reach out and comfort him. To offer the solace he had given to her. He must have fretted and stewed during the long hours of Angie's surgery, wondering if he would ever see his daughter again, fearing the worst and regretting his decision to let her jump on the trampoline. Emma wished she had been here with him.

"You deserve a good man to love you, Emma. I'm sure you'll find him some day." He brushed a hand across his face and she heard the rasp of his unshaven chin.

Everything about his body language told her he didn't want her here. But when she looked into his eyes, she saw a depth of emotion that cried out for her to stay. Inside, she was screaming. "I understand."

But she didn't, not really.

"I'll see you sometime," he said dismissively.

He was pushing her away.

"Will you...will you tell Angie goodbye for me?" she asked.

"Yeah, I'll tell her. Thanks for taking the time to come down here to see Angie. I appreciate your concern."

His words poured over her like a bucket of ice water. A horrible feeling settled in the pit of her stomach.

Please don't send me away.

He moved back and looked at Angie.

Emma's spine stiffened and she couldn't keep the hurt from her voice. "Mark, I'm not just one of Angie's doctors. I'm—I'm—"

An outsider. She should leave.

Horrible, swelling silence followed. He wouldn't look at her. A clatter sounded outside the door and a nurse came in carrying a tray. When Mark turned to look at Emma, she was gone.

Just like that, she was out of his life.

Tension filled his body. Emma had left, taking all happiness with her. He felt miserable and lost, but believed it was for the best.

Shaking his head, he went to sit near Angie, taking solace in watching her sleep. She needed stability and his full attention. She didn't need more hurt.

Neither did Emma.

As he gazed at his precious daughter's face, the emptiness persisted. He tried to ignore the doubt that he had just lost one of the two best things in his life.

Chapter Twenty-One

Emma slipped out of the intensive care unit and hurried down the hallway. Several people stood waiting for the elevator. She ducked her head and veered past as she ran for the stairs. Inside the stairwell, the door slammed behind her, echoing through the hollow recesses of her soul.

Alone on the landing, she leaned back against the white brick wall and squeezed her eyes shut. Tears ran down her cheeks. She didn't even try to brush them away.

Gone!

She had lost two more people she loved so dearly and the pain was almost more than she could stand. In many ways, it almost hurt more than when Brian had died. Brian had not wanted to leave her, but he'd had no choice. Mark was still very much alive, yet he didn't want her. There was nothing she could do to convince him otherwise.

A sob wrenched from her throat as she slid down the wall and hunkered in the corner of the landing. Burying her face in her hands, she gave way to the flow of despair.

"Father in Heaven," she whispered in a hoarse voice. "Why has this happened? Am I so unlovable? I was so certain that Mark and I had a future. How could I have been so wrong?"

Be at peace. I have not left you. All things are within My control.

The words brought small comfort to Emma's heart and she uttered a simple prayer. "I'll do whatever You want me to do, Lord, but does it have to hurt so bad? Haven't I known enough suffering?"

A peaceful feeling crept over her, enfolding her with warmth.

You have learned, but now it is Mark's turn to learn to trust Me.

She didn't understand. Mark's faith seemed so strong. He stood firm even when his wife deserted him, even when Angie got sick.

Emma sniffed and wiped her nose. An overwhelming tranquility filled her to overflowing, a sweet energy that was so compelling she could shed no more tears. It had taken so long for her to regain her faith in God. To be able to return to the pediatric intensive care floor of the hospital. It gave her confidence and renewed her hope and strength. God loved her, she knew that without reservation. He had a specific plan for her, though He might not have revealed it to her yet. Deep inside, she felt such peace, it filled her to overflowing.

She would accept whatever He had planned for her.

Standing, she dug into her purse for a tissue, then blew her nose. She would be patient and put her life in God's hands. He would care for her. She must believe that He would care for Mark and Angie, too.

* * *

One month later, Angie sat on the edge of the mattress in her bedroom. She squeezed the teddy bear Emma had given her the day of the Make-A-Wish barbecue.

"But I don't want to go to San Francisco again, Dad. I want to go back to Emma for my chemo injections."

Angie rested her chin on top of Teddy's head and scowled at her father.

Mark sighed as he hung clothes in her closet. Tired and cranky, he didn't want to fight with her. "You know Emma isn't your doctor anymore, Angie. It's best for you if we go to Dr. Walton at U.C.S.F. He's been doing okay for you, hasn't he?"

Angie pursed her lips. "Yeah, but I don't like Dr. Walton. He smells bad and has yellow teeth."

"He smells like antiseptic, Angie. That's how doctors smell."

"Not Emma."

No, not Emma. She smelled like a delicate flower on a warm spring day.

"I want to go see Emma, Dad. I miss her. Why don't you like her anymore?"

His emotions churned inside him, like a volcano gearing up for an eruption. How could he explain all the complexities to Angie when he didn't understand them himself? He only knew what he felt.

I love her.

The revelation wasn't new to Mark, though he tried to deny it.

Pulling back the covers of Angie's bed, he urged her to crawl between the sheets. Then, he sat next to her, feeling the clinging warmth of her hand tucked within his. "I like Dr. Shields just fine, honey. But I believe Dr. Walton is better for us now."

Angie sniffed, rubbing her face against Teddy's fur. She glanced at the picture of her mother sitting on the bedside table. "I thought…I thought if I had another mommy, you'd be happy again."

"Honey, I have you. I am happy."

She shook her head. "No, you're not. You never laugh anymore. Emma makes us cookies and plays with us. Mom never did those things. You started to smile again when we were with Emma. You can't just leave her, Dad. You have to marry her. She's ours."

Mark didn't reply. His throat closed and he couldn't speak.

"You know, Dad, I love Mom. But I love Emma, too. And she treats us better than Mom does."

"Yeah, I know," he agreed, surprised once more by her grown-up insight. "How'd you get to be so smart?"

She smiled, showing a new front tooth that had almost grown back after the baby tooth had fallen out. "Well, you've always told me I have Mom's beauty and your brains."

At the mention of Denise, he realized he hadn't heard from her since he'd sent Emma away, just after Angie's last surgery. Angie had stopped asking to visit her mother. Instead she asked for Emma. Even after two months, the child wouldn't let it drop.

"Please take me to see Emma."

"I've already told you no," he answered gently.

Angie opened her mouth again and Mark placed his fingers against her lips. "No more arguing, young lady. Go to sleep. I'm doing what I think is best for all of us."

Bending down, he tried to kiss her forehead, but she jerked a blanket over her head. Though she was a child, her rejection cut him deep.

He hugged her instead, finding her body stiff and unyielding. Regardless, she felt good to him, so warm, so alive. He'd made the right choice. By staying away from Emma, he protected all of them from being hurt any more than necessary.

Doubt crowded his mind, but he pushed it aside. No matter what, he would never stop loving Emma. He carried her in his heart and knew he'd never let her go.

Mark stood and walked to the door where he turned off the light. "I love you, Angie."

"I love you, too, Dad. And I love Emma." Angie's muffled whisper reached across the darkened room.

"I know, honey. I miss her, too."

The confession broke through his defenses and he walked out before he said something else he might regret. Though he had admitted to himself that he loved Emma, he hadn't spoken the words out loud. As long as he didn't vocalize his feelings, he could keep them from being true.

Or could he?

In the kitchen, he put the milk away and loaded the dishwasher. His gaze drifted over to the telephone. Before he knew what he was doing, he lifted the receiver and dialed Emma's number, then hung up before it rang. It felt like years since he'd seen her.

Was she still attending the Make-A-Wish advisory meetings? Because of Angie's latest recovery and the long drives to receive her treatments at U.C.S.F., Mark didn't have time to attend the meetings anymore. He missed the association with the Make-A-Wish people. Maybe he should resign. It would be difficult working with Emma without telling her he loved her and wanted her near.

Shaking his head, he tried to get her out of his mind. In the family room, he found the remote control and slouched on the couch as he switched on the television. He scanned channels, looking for something to take his mind off Dr. Emma Shields.

It was no use. The sound of her voice, her laugh and the scent of her hair filled his mind.

He flipped off the TV. Maybe he should go to bed, but he didn't have the energy to walk up the stairs. Numbing sadness encased his entire being.

He closed his eyes and leaned his head back. The vision of her lovely face swam before him, the slight dimple in her right cheek when she gave him a stunning smile. No matter what he did, she was there, inside his heart.

He snorted. "Ah, come on!"

Impatient, he shot off the couch and went upstairs to his bedroom, then got ready for bed in the dark. It was late and he had to get Angie up early so they could drive to San Francisco.

Busying himself with tidying up the bathroom, he refused to think of Emma. He was successful—for about thirty seconds.

Before he got into bed, he fell to his knees in his nightly ritual of prayer. This time, no words would come. He felt empty inside, hollow and all alone.

Why do you want Emma out of your life? Don't push her away. You and Angie need her.

The words filled his mind.

"Heavenly Father, I can't ask her to go through this struggle with Angie. It wouldn't be fair."

Emma is stronger than you think.

"But I don't want Angie hurt, either. Emma is a distraction that keeps me from focusing on Angie's needs."

A distraction that keeps you from loving and being hurt again?

"Yes!"

Mark groaned. He was talking to himself. But, the spirit whispered the truth. He feared being hurt again.

He clasped his hands as he pressed his forehead against the mattress. When he first married Denise, he thought he loved her. Later, after Angie was born, he knew he loved her. She was his wife and the mother of his child, after all.

And she had never returned that sentiment. He meant nothing more to her than a sugar daddy, someone to give her a great lifestyle. He couldn't fault her. In the beginning, he'd sought the same things. But somehow, his feelings had changed over time.

When Denise left, it nearly destroyed him. Angie provided a needed distraction from the pain of the divorce. Loving Emma reminded him of all he had lost and all he could lose again.

He had sent Emma away, treading on her feelings as brutally as a bulldozer. Because he was frightened of what she made him feel. Frightened of being hurt again. He had preached to Emma about the healing power of forgiveness and God's love, yet he couldn't bring himself to practice those same principles.

What a hypocrite.

Shame heated his face when he realized what he had

done. Shaking his head, he climbed onto the bed and lay on top of the covers. He welcomed the breeze from the open window, but it did little to cool his humiliation.

"What have I done?" he whispered to the night. "And how can I ever repair the damage?"

He closed his eyes. A vision of Emma smiling flooded his mind and he tossed and turned most of the night.

Chapter Twenty-Two

The next day Angie wouldn't eat breakfast. Or lunch. Even the Marinol didn't help this time.

They had just come from her chemo injection and Mark blamed that. Deep inside, he knew better. Angie missed Emma.

So did he.

Sitting in the hospital cafeteria, he tried to get her to eat something before they went to their one o'clock MRI appointment. He had put EMLA Cream on her arm where they would administer the dye, but it didn't seem to matter. Two needle pokes in one day wasn't fun no matter how much the ELMA Cream dulled the pain.

Angie didn't even pick up her turkey-and-cheese sandwich. She stared out the wide windows of the cafeteria, watching people walk by, ignoring the hum of chatter and the clinking of dishes.

Glancing at his own tuna sandwich, Mark couldn't blame her. He didn't have much of an appetite, either. And yet, if he couldn't get her to eat, she'd lose more weight and—

"You're not hungry?" he asked, forcing himself to take a bite and chew.

Angie shook her head. Over the last month, it seemed they had both lost their zest for life. Angie's eyes no longer sparkled and she rarely found a reason to laugh.

Not since the day of the barbecue.

I'm losing Angie. She's wasting away right before my eyes.

All things considered, she was alive and doing fine, but she didn't care anymore. She had quit trying. And that scared him most of all.

"Come on, let's go get your MRI over with." Mark stacked their plates on a tray and carried them over to the dishwasher conveyer belt.

Angie followed, her head hung low as she took his hand and followed him down the expansive hallway.

Inside the diagnostic center, Mark helped Angie remove her bracelet. Because of the magnetic force, she couldn't wear anything with metal during her MRI.

"You ready?" Bill, their technician, asked in a cheerful tone.

Angie nodded and followed Bill into the MRI room. The deafening whoosh of the machine hurt Angie's ears and Bill helped her put plugs in.

Once they prepped Angie for her MRI, she laid flat on her back and a nurse administered the dye. Angie clasped Mark's hand, tears brimming her eyes.

"I wish Emma were here." She spoke in a quivering voice, her face ashen. "It never hurts as much when Emma's here."

A lump rose in Mark's throat and he tried to swallow. While he was falling head-over-heels in love with

Emma Shields, his little daughter had done the same thing. He shouldn't be surprised.

Bill slid Angie into the tubelike machine. Angie was so used to it by now that she never got claustrophobic or moved around in the confined space. If she did, they'd have to poke her with another needle to administer a sedative, which provided great incentive to lie very still.

"Okay, Mr. Williams, if you'll come outside with me, we can start the scan."

Mark followed Bill into the observation room, then stared over the technician's shoulder at the computer screen. Layer upon layer, Bill scanned Angie's brain. Mark didn't feel optimistic as his gaze searched the screen and found the hazy white spot of the brain tumor. It looked smaller, but he couldn't be sure.

"Can you tell if the tumor has shrunk?" Mark asked, unable to contain the anxiousness in his tone.

"I'm sorry, Mr. Williams," Bill answered, "but I really need to let your neurosurgeon look at the scans. He'll give you his report."

Mark sighed as he stared at Bill's poker face. Lawsuits were too prevalent and, even though the technician saw hundreds of these scans every week, Bill would never speak out of turn and render a verdict. An hour later, Mark and Angie sat in Dr. Meacham's office, waiting for him to review the scans and offer his opinion. Mark squeezed his clammy hands together, wishing the doctor would hurry up.

Several times, Dr. Meacham measured the scans with a ruler, comparing the current set of scans with the ones they had taken each month over the past six months.

"Incredible," Dr. Meacham murmured under his

breath as he squinted at the scans illuminated in the lighted trays hanging on the wall.

"What do you see?" Tingles of hope coursed through Mark's arms and legs, and he felt Angie shift restlessly by his side. She was anxious for good news, too.

Dr. Meacham faced Mark, his expression one of utter disbelief. "It's a miracle, Mark. I've been practicing medicine for years, and I have *never* seen this much shrinkage for this type of brain tumor. Never!"

"What?" Mark shot out of his chair and came to stand next to the doctor in front of the wall.

Angie scooted forward onto the edge of her chair, her eyes wide and sparkling.

"Show me," Mark demanded. His gaze skipped across the myriad scans.

"See here?" Dr. Meacham pointed at a white spot on several separate scans. "That's the tumor." Then, he held up the ruler and measured before he pointed at another scan. "This is the MRI taken last month."

The doctor moved the ruler to measure the tumor. "This is the same view of today's scan. Since we started Angie's chemo protocol, the tumor has shrunken approximately fifty-five percent. The most we expected by the end of Angie's protocol was twenty percent. It's amazing, Mark, but this shows a fifty-five percent shrinkage. Angie's tumor is in remission. Obviously the protocol we have her on is working very well, and you owe it all to Dr. Shields."

"Dr. Shields?" Mark's mouth dropped open.

"Yes, she called to confer with me about five months ago when it appeared Angie's current protocol wasn't affecting the tumor. Dr. Shields suggested a new combination of drugs. At first, I was skeptical, but then I thought it over. I wouldn't have approved the change if I didn't believe it would work. I'm sure glad I agreed. I have no doubt the Tumor Board will be happy to hear about this breakthrough."

Emma had done this? Because of Emma, Angie's tumor was in remission.

Joy trembled in Mark's chest and he laughed out loud. "Whoopee!"

He reached for Angie, pulling her into his arms, hugging her tight as he whirled her about the room. "Did you hear that, Angie-babe? The tumor has shrunk fifty-five percent. The most Dr. Meacham has ever seen!"

"That's over half, Dad." Angie's happy giggle sent a shiver of delight over him.

"Yes, my smart girl. Over half gone." Mark kissed his daughter's cheek.

Dr. Meacham grinned as he dropped the ruler into the pocket of his white jacket. "Well, you have good reason to celebrate. We need to be cautious, but this is tremendous news."

"We have to tell Emma. Can we take the scans to her office and show her today?" Angie's eyes sparkled.

It had been so long since Mark had seen his daughter this happy. One long, harrowing month since he had felt like laughing. Yet, his feelings were a riot of unease. What if Angie took a turn for the worse? "Uh, it will be quite late by the time we drive back to Reno, honey."

"Well, if you see Dr. Shields, tell her I said hello." Dr. Meacham started pulling the scans out of the lighted trays and placing them in their envelope. "I knew when I referred you to Dr. Shields she'd be good for you two."

"What do you mean?" An uneasy feeling settled in Mark's stomach.

"I went to med school with Emma and I know how hard her son's death was on her. She quit taking pediatric patients because of it. For some reason, I felt strongly that I should refer you to her for Angie's oncology, though I'm not certain why." Dr. Meacham shook his head.

Doubt clouded Mark's mind. In the beginning, he had been so certain God had led him to Emma, to help Angie. Could there be more to it than that? Maybe Emma had needed *him* as much as he and Angie had needed her. Yet, Mark had pushed her away just when they had come to realize how much they meant to one another.

Just when he had fallen in love with her.

Larry stepped toward the door. "I'm going to get back to work. I know you have a long trip ahead of you. Don't forget to stop along the way and celebrate."

"Thank you, Dr. Meacham." Mark shook the doctor's hand. "Thanks for everything."

Emma took a deep, steadying breath as she walked toward the front reception counter of her medical office. Thank goodness she was finished for the day. She couldn't concentrate. Instead of focusing on what her patients were saying, she found herself thinking about Mark and Angie, wondering how they were doing, hoping Angie was getting better.

Emma longed to call Mark. She wished she dared make homemade cookies and take them over to their house. It wouldn't be proper.

He didn't want her.

Standing at the reception counter, Emma jotted notes on the last patient's file for the day. Darcy sat at the counter with Tom leaning over the top as they tried to clarify a delivery of blood samples before they left for the evening.

Emma prepared to enter her office where she planned to make a few phone calls and complete a mountain of paperwork before she went home to her lonely apartment.

Tomorrow, she had a Make-A-Wish meeting. They were planning a new fund-raiser, with her as team leader.

Sunday, she had church. Because she played the piano, they had asked her to begin directing the children at singing time and the possibilities excited her. Her congregation had welcomed her with open arms, eager to involve her.

Extracurricular activities now filled her life. She was having a blast, and yet a part of her remained vacant because she missed Mark and Angie. She didn't feel whole. She hoped she would get over them sometime soon, but doubted it. Love wasn't something she could turn on and off that easily.

"Dr. Shields?"

Emma glanced at Sonja. "Yes?"

Sonja inclined her head toward the outer door of the reception room. "I think you have a visitor."

Emma glanced that way and her mouth dropped open. "Angie!"

Angie Williams stood in the reception room, holding a large bouquet of red long-stemmed roses. Emma almost fell over.

The little girl stared at Emma, dimples showing on her smiling face.

"Hi, Angie," Sonja greeted the girl. "We've sure missed you. How are you doing, kiddo?"

"Fine, thanks." Angie smiled at Sonja before her gaze returned to Emma.

"Who are the flowers for?" Sonja asked, her eyes twinkling with mischief.

"They're for Emma." Angie walked toward the doctor.

For me?

Emma could hardly believe it. The room spun around her and she tried to focus.

Angie thrust the flowers at her and Emma held them dumbly, her hands shaking. "These are for you, Emma, for taking such good care of me. Won't you forgive Dad for being stupid and come home with us? We miss you."

Kids had such a simple way of looking at things. They always spoke their minds.

A lead weight settled in Emma's chest. She knelt and hugged Angie, crushing the fragrant roses between them. "Oh, Angie, there's nothing to forgive."

Emma could feel Angie's little hands clutching her shoulders, squeezing tight. It felt so good to hold this child, to see her, hear her, touch her once more.

"I love my mom, but I want you to be my mom, too, Emma," Angie whispered. "Come home with us, please."

Questions raced through Emma's mind. What about Mark? Her heart plummeted. She wanted to be with Mark and Angie more than anything, but Mark didn't—

They drew apart, just a bit. Emma wiped her eyes as she gazed at Angie. "Are you here alone? Where's your father?"

A movement at the doorway caught her eye and she looked up. Mark leaned against the threshold, dressed impeccably in a dark double-breasted suit. His slicked-back sand-colored hair framed a charming smile gracing his masculine face. His gaze locked with hers as he sauntered toward her with fluid grace. She was vaguely aware of her staff members standing by the counter, watching in silence. Every one of them wore a cheesy grin.

Tremors of delight spiraled through her. Just seeing him again lit up her soul like the Fourth of July.

Taking Emma's hands in his, Mark helped her stand and Angie backed away, grinning. Emma stared in disbelief, forcing herself to take a breath.

"Tell her about the tumor, Dad," Angie whispered loudly.

Emma glanced between them. "What's going on?"

He shook his head, his eyes filled with amazement. "You didn't tell me you spoke to Dr. Meacham five months ago about changing Angie's chemo protocol."

"Well, I didn't think—"

He gave a throaty laugh. "It worked, Emma. The tumor has shrunk by over fifty-five percent."

"What?" She laughed, too, hardly able to believe it.

"Do you know what this means?" Mark asked.

Nodding, Emma cleared her throat but still spoke in a tight squeak. "Yes, it means there's still four months left on the protocol and the tumor should shrink even more before she's through. Angie will be in a group of less than one percent of children for survivorship with her type of brain tumor. It means that—"

God had not let her down.

Emma's heart swelled with joy. Her Heavenly Father had worked a miracle for them. He'd been there beside them through everything. How foolish not to recognize

His loving presence in her life, even during her darkest hours. She hadn't seen it, but somehow He had made everything right. For her, and for Mark and Angie.

"How can I ever thank you, Emma?" Mark asked. "I'll be forever in your debt."

"I can't take credit for this, Mark. I asked God for help and He told me what to do. It's kind of hard to explain, but He did this, not me."

Emotion played across his face. "What a miracle the Lord has wrought in our lives."

"Yes," she agreed. "I—I don't know what to say."

Mark went down on one knee, gazing up into her eyes with adoration. "Say you'll be mine, Emma. Marry me. I can't promise there won't be difficult times ahead, but I can promise I'll stand beside you through it all. I don't want to be without you anymore. Neither does Angie."

She stared as he reached into his pants' pocket and withdrew a diamond ring, holding it up for her inspection. The glittering stone winked at her and she blinked to clear the tears from her eyes. This was a dream come true.

"I haven't been able to get you off my mind." His deep voice filled the room, the only sound she heard. "I'm so sorry for hurting you. I thought I was protecting you by sending you away. Now, I realize we'd both be stronger if we're together. How can we be strong when we're apart?"

"Protecting me? I've been miserable."

"So have I. Please forgive me. I love you, Emma Shields. I love you more than I can say."

Adoration shimmered in his eyes, mirroring her own overpowering emotions. Tears ran down her cheeks but she ignored them. What were a few tears when the man you loved made a statement like that?

"Mark—" she croaked, barely able to speak.

"Marry us, Emma! Say yes," Angie yelled, jumping up and down with excitement.

Christy wiped tears from her cheeks while Sonja joined Angie's chorus. "Say yes, Emma. Say yes!"

Emma hesitated, just to savor this remarkable moment. Just to cherish the miracle of God's love.

"Oh, yes! Yes, I'll marry you. I'd rather go through any pain than go on living without you. I love you and Angie so much."

She found herself wrapped tight in Mark's arms. His strength surrounded her, his deep laughter ringing in her ears.

"I thought I'd lost you," she whispered against his neck.

"Never!"

Angie joined them, clasping Emma's legs until Mark leaned down and picked her up. They embraced in a huddle and no words were needed. Their laughter and sighs of elation spoke volumes.

Tears of happiness dripped from Emma's eyes. She had found her place of belonging, a place of healing. It was here, wrapped in the arms of her new family and God's redeeming love. She had been so lost, but now she was found.

"Come on," Mark said. "Let's go home."

* * * * *

Dear Reader,

One of the greatest nightmares a parent can face is for their child to suffer a life-threatening illness. Unfortunately my family and I lived the research for this book. In 1998, our beautiful seven-year-old daughter was diagnosed with an inoperable brain tumor. After six surgeries, a year of chemotherapy, and numerous other traumas, our neurosurgeon advised us our daughter was the top child in the world for survivorship of her type of brain tumor. But not all children are so blessed.

We never know when a loved one might be stricken with a serious illness. How easy it is during our darkest hours to blame God. When He walked the earth, the Savior performed miracles among mankind. I am convinced He continues to work wonders in the world today, in your life and in mine. When we seek Him and look for the good, we can see the hand of the Lord everywhere, working on our behalf. If this story inspires you to never, ever give up hope and to cling to the Lord for sustenance through all your troubles, then I will have accomplished my goal.

I invite you to visit my Web site at www.LeighBale.com to learn more about how you can help children suffering with a critical illness and to read more about my books.

May you each cherish your loved ones and enjoy health and strength during the years ahead!

Leigh Bale

QUESTIONS FOR DISCUSSION

1. In The Healing Place, all three of the main characters—Emma, Mark and Angie—are in need of healing. Some of their infirmities are physical, some are spiritual and emotional. How does each character deal with his or hear particular weakness? Does this change throughout the story?

2. At one time, Mark thought of nothing but wealth, prestige and worldly possessions. Why did his priorities change? How do you think this affected his ability to cope with his divorce and daughter's critical illness?

3. After Emma's son died, she blamed God. How did Mark's faith help change Emma's perspective? How was she finally able to make peace with her Heavenly Father? Have you had difficult experiences in your own life when you were tempted to blame God? How did you make peace with God? What impact did your resolutions have on your life?

4. Emma's ex-husband blamed her for their child's death, which led her to feel racked by guilt. How did this change her relationship with God and others around her? Has guilt ever eaten away at your heart? How did you overcome this pain?

5. When Make-A-Wish asked Emma to serve on their advisory committee, she agreed even though she

felt inadequate. What does that decision say about her character? Can you think of a time in your life when you felt inadequate to serve others? How did you find the courage to overcome your reticence? Can you think of some examples in your own life when a friend or loved one has served you during a difficult time in your life? How did their support make a difference?

6. Both Mark and Emma came from broken marriages. What trust issues might this cause in a future relationship? How did Mark and Emma overcome this? Can you think of any advice for someone in a situation like this?

7. In high school, Mark felt drawn to Emma enough to confide his most secret dreams to her. What good qualities do you think Emma had that Mark felt drawn to her even though he ended up dumping her for another? What bad qualities in Mark helped drive them apart? How might these qualities hinder or benefit a relationship or marriage?

8. We know God is all-powerful and all-loving. Why does He allow suffering to exist on earth? How does He help us overcome our trials and tribulations?

9. In spite of her illness, Angie worried over her father's sadness and tried to find ways to help him be happy. Compare how God also wants us to be happy. Can you think of ways God has worked to help you be happy in your life?

10. At the end of the book, Mark pushed Emma away, yet she continued to exercise her faith in God even though she had been hurt once more. How did she have the strength to remain firm in her faith in this time? Why is it important to acknowledge our dependence on God? How does this acknowledgment influence our approach to life? Discuss ways that walking by faith can help us grow spiritually.

LOVE INSPIRED HISTORICAL

Powerful, engaging stories of romance, adventure and faith set in the past—when life was simpler and faith played a major role in everyday lives.

There was something about the young woman—something he couldn't put his finger on. He'd hardly glanced at her when he'd hauled her from the family sleigh, but now he took a longer look through the veil of falling snow.

For a moment her silhouette, her size and her movements all reminded him of Noelle. How about that. Noelle, his frozen heart reminded him with a painful squeeze, had been his first—and only—love.

It couldn't be her, he reasoned, since she was married and probably a mother by now. She'd be safe in town, living snugly in one of the finest houses in the county instead of riding along the country roads in a storm. Still, curiosity nibbled at him, and he plowed through the knee deep snow. Snow was falling faster now, and yet somehow through the thick downfall his gaze seemed to find her.

She was fragile, a delicate bundle of wool—and snow clung to her hood and scarf and cloak like a shroud, making her tough to see. She'd been just a little bit of a thing when he'd lifted her from the sleigh, and his only thought at the time had been to get both women out of danger. Now something chewed at his memory. He couldn't quite figure out what, but he could feel it in his gut.

The woman was talking on as she unwound her niece's veil. "We were tossed about dreadfully. You're likely bruised and broken from root to stem. I've never been so terrified. All I could do was pray over and over and think of you, my dear." Her words warmed with tenderness. "What a greater nightmare for you."

"We're fine. All's well that ends well," the niece insisted.

Although her voice was muffled by the thick snowfall, his step faltered. There *was* something about her voice, something familiar in the gentle resonance of her alto. Now he could see the top part of her face, due to her loosened scarf. Her eyes—they were a startling, flawless emerald green.

Whoa, there. He'd seen that perfect shade of green before—and long ago. Recognition speared through his midsection, but he already knew she was his Noelle even before the last layer of the scarf fell away from her face.

His Noelle, just as lovely and dear, was now blind and veiled with snow. His first love. The woman he'd spent years and thousands of miles trying to forget. Hard to believe that there she was suddenly right in front of him. He'd heard about the engagement announcement a few years back, and he'd known in returning to live Angel Falls that he'd have to run into her eventually.

He just didn't figure it would be so soon and like this.

Seeing her again shouldn't make him feel as if he'd been hit in the chest with a cannonball. The shock was wearing off, he realized, the same as when you received a hard blow. First off, you were too stunned to feel it. Then the pain began to settle in, just a hint, and then rushing in until it was unbearable. Yep, that was the word to describe what was happening inside his rib cage. A pain worse than a broken bone beat through him.

Best get the sleigh righted, the horse hitched back up and the women home. But it was all he could to do turn his back as he took his mustang by the bridle. The palomino pinto gave him a snort and shook his head, sending the snow on his golden mane flying.

I know how you feel, Sunny, Thad thought. Judging by the look of things, it would be a long time until they had a chance to get in out of the cold.

He'd do best to ignore the women, especially Noelle, and to get to the work needin' to be done. He gave the sleigh a shove, but the vehicle was wedged against the snow-covered brush banking the river. Not that he'd put a lot of weight on the Lord over much these days, but Thad had to admit it was a close call. Almost eerie how he'd caught them just in time. It did seem providential. Had they gone only a few feet more, gravity would have done the trick and pulled the sleigh straight into the frigid, fast waters of Angel River and plummeted them directly over the tallest falls in the territory.

Thad squeezed his eyes shut. He couldn't stand to think of Noelle tossed into that river, fighting the powerful current along with the ice chunks. There would have been no way to have pulled her from the river in time. Had he been a few minutes slower in coming after them or if Sunny hadn't been so swift, there would have been no way to save her. To fate, to the Lord or to simple chance, he was grateful.

Some tiny measure of tenderness in his chest, like a fire long banked, sputtered to life. His tenderness for her, still there, after so much time and distance. How about that.

Since the black gelding was a tad calmer now that the sound of the train had faded off into the distance, Thad rehitched him to the sleigh but secured the driving reins to his saddle horn. He used the two horses working together to free the sleigh and get it realigned toward the road.

The older woman looked uncertain about getting back into the vehicle. With the way that black gelding of theirs was twitchy and wild-eyed, he didn't blame her. "Don't worry, ma'am, I'll see you two ladies home."

"Th-that would be very good of you, sir. I'm rather shaken up. I've half a mind to walk the entire mile home, except for my dear niece."

Noelle. He wouldn't let his heart react to her. All that mattered was doing right by her—and that was one thing that hadn't changed. He came around to help the aunt into the sleigh and after she was safely seated, turned toward Noelle. Her scarf had slid down to reveal the curve of her face, the slope of her nose and the rosebud smile of her mouth.

What had happened to her? How had she lost her sight? Sadness filled him for her blindness and for what could have been between them, once. He thought about saying something to her, so she would know who he was, but what good would that do? The past was done and over. Only the emptiness of it remained.

"Thank you so much, sir." She turned toward the sound of his step and smiled in his direction. If she, too, wondered who he was, she gave no real hint of it.

He didn't expect her to. Chances were she hardly remembered him, and if she did, she wouldn't think too well of him. She would never know what good wishes he wanted for her as he took her gloved hand. The layers of wool and leather and sheepskin lining between his hand and hers didn't stop that tiny flame of tenderness for her in his chest from growing a notch.

He looked into her eyes, into Noelle's eyes, the woman he'd loved truly so long ago, knowing she did not recognize him. Could not see him or sense him, even at heart. She smiled at him as if he were the Good Samaritan she thought he was as he helped her settle onto the seat.

Love was an odd thing, he realized as he backed away. Once, their love had been an emotion felt so strong and pure and true that he would have vowed on his very soul that nothing could tarnish nor diminish their bond. But time had done that simply, easily, and they stood now as strangers.

* * * * *

Don't miss this deeply moving
Love Inspired Historical story about
a young woman in 1883 Montana who reunites
with an old beau and soon discovers that
love is the greatest blessing of all.

Love Inspired®

TITLES AVAILABLE NEXT MONTH

Don't miss these four stories in January

FAMILY IN HIS HEART by Gail Gaymer Martin
Nick Thornton could tell Rona Meyers was a special person, so he'd offered her a much-needed job. And as he got to know her, he couldn't stop wondering if God was offering him a new beginning and a second chance at love.

NEXT DOOR DADDY by Debra Clopton
A Mule Hollow novel
When rancher Nate Talbert prayed for a change to his reclusive life, he got new next-door neighbor Pollyanna McDonald. But the menagerie of pets that she and her son cared for was driving him *crazy.* Could he handle the chaos that surrounded her?

THE DOCTOR'S BRIDE by Patt Marr
Everyone in town was trying to find Dr. Zack Hemingway a wife. Yet the one girl who caught his eye wasn't interested. Why was Chloe Kilgannon hiding from him? This doctor knew it would take some good medicine to get to the heart of the matter.

A SOLDIER'S PROMISE by Cheryl Wyatt
Wings of Refuge
Pararescue jumper Joel Montgomery had the power to make a sick little boy's dream come true. He was determined to follow through even if it meant returning to a place he'd rather forget. And meeting the boy's pretty teacher made his leap of faith doubly worth the price.

LICNM1207